THE PROBLEM WITH PIXIES

HOMESTEADER HEARTH WITCH
BOOK ONE

KAT HEALY

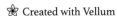 Created with Vellum

for Scott, Shari, and Ame

Magic is out there. Go find it.

CHAPTER ONE

THE FARMHOUSE WAS INFESTED WITH PIXIES.

You didn't see them peeking out from behind the lacy wisps of seemingly moth-eaten curtains, nor snatched glimpses of them in the gloomy cracks between the porch's warped floorboards. It was the entire look of the place, like the old farmhouse and its decrepit garden were clinging to the life of one final breath before finally, begrudgingly, submitting to an existence of neglect.

I loved it.

Anything old, ancient, anything with memories and secrets. A dusty attic filled with rusty-latched trunks that hadn't been open in decades? Bring up a bottle of Riesling and call me a cheap date.

Growing up in the family of hearth witches of Hawthorne Manor also gave me an appreciation for horticulture, so my fingers were positively itching to get that weedy garden under control. Instead, they restrained themselves and jangled the squeaky garden gate loose. I had to aid its opening with a shove of my foot against the tall grass, but then I was sweeping up the overgrown path to the front porch.

The planks were still strong, resilient. *That makes two of us.*

I set my mini potted plant down on the nearest windowsill and pressed a hand against the chipped paint of the front door. "Hey, old girl."

The old iron key was warm from being inside my pocket, the address label attached by its little keyring still declaring: *The Pembertons, 1749 Apple Blossom Lane, Redbud Indiana.* After wiggling the address label free, I stuck it in my back pocket. There was a similar declaration over the doorbell, so I pulled that little slip of cardstock free with my fingernail, turned it over, and wrote *Misty Fields.* This place had had enough old memories. It was time for new ones.

Inserting the key into the lock, I gave it a twist. "Let's get us both cleaned up, okay, old girl?"

Two days on the run for me and what seemed like over two decades of neglect for the farmhouse had both made us a little scruffy.

My magic came easily to my fingertips, flashing a muted pulse of green light from under my palm. Even though it was a mild expenditure of magic, the parasite ring on my middle finger absorbed most of it, leaving but a remnant for the house. Still, it was enough to seal my solemn promise, and the old farmhouse seemed to sigh. Not in resignation, but in relief. The front door opened without even a squeak.

As much as I wanted to explore, first things first. I raced through the house, making as much noise as I could with my feet pounding up the stairs and across the floorboards, and flung aside every curtain and opened every window and door, even the vents in the attic.

Pixies were fair flyers, but they were absolute rubbish when it came to navigating a crosswind. If there were any more secreted away, this was sure to flush them out. The weather was fair, on the cusp of autumn, and the breezes that came with the change in season swept through the house, along with a fair amount of yellowing leaves from the big sugar maple on the south side of the garden. I didn't care. Those could all be cleared away.

"Just like these spider webs," I declared loudly, planting my hands on my hips. The new queen of this house had arrived. "Y'all been given notice, spiders. Time to move out or make new homes I'll never find. I don't like walking into your webs and I know you don't like rebuilding them, so shake all eight of those legs and get to it."

There was a gentle skittering sound, no more than a whisper, as the spiders hurried to obey the new witch who'd taken up residence. One particularly white garden spider missing a leg struggled to vacate its home above the kitchen sink. Retrieving a leaf from the floor, I gently swept the spider from its haphazard web and deposited it on the windowsill. "There you go. Bye now."

After testing the stove and running the well water from every faucet until it was no longer rusty brown but sweet and clear, I left the doors and windows open and returned to the car. The average new homeowner would have excitedly unloaded her car, quickly claiming the farmhouse as her own, but I knew better. You never left luggage or personal belongings unattended if there were pixies loose. They weren't malevolent, just mischievous, but such mischievous behavior, if left unchecked, could attract *other* mischievous things. Bigger, nastier things.

I glanced down at the bandages thickening my left forearm under the sleeve. The Big Nasty had even left a claw behind, lodged in the iron cuff I wore around my wrist. I wore two, one on each wrist, and had been trained to use them against the fae, or any others that meant me harm. Legend said us supes— witches, shifters, vampires, and everything in between—had been born of fae magic, adapted to this Earthly realm. The fae

3

said we'd stolen it, perverted it, and you never knew when someone with a centuries-old grudge might take it out on you.

That Big Nasty had been fae, though not the kind I'd been trained to fight, and I'd thanked the Green Mother *and* all my lucky stars I'd gotten away with just a mangled arm and a claw embedded in my cuff. Had it been a tooth... well, I'd be six feet underground. Or worse.

Cursed.

I might be that already, courtesy of my grandmother. But when I was younger and naïve, she'd told me I was strong, even by Hawthorne standards, so maybe I could withstand her magic.

She hadn't sent a tracker after me yet—Redbud was still standing.

And there was no smell of sulfur in the air, so there weren't any hellhounds to worry about, yet.

She didn't know where I was, thanks to my Vanishing Spell and the parasite ring that reduced my magical signature to that of an average green witch, but the pixies could change that.

"First things first, second things second," I reminded myself. And that was pixie-proofing my new haven before sundown.

They'd all fled at the sound of my car driving up the gravel lot that morning, but they'd be back. And curious. And curious creatures stuck their noses into places where they didn't belong. Found hidden things. I loved a good secret, a hidden keepsake, as much as the next curious individual, but even I knew when something should just remain forgotten.

I'd have to make my trip into town quick.

The little town of Redbud had a rotary square with four roads that shuttled me off to its primary businesses: Galloway's Grocery and its adjoining liquor market simply named Cold Beer, the little diner called Patty's, local plant nursery Flora's Garden Dreams, and to the west, the hardware store Hammer &

Nails and a massive red barn converted from its hay-storing days into a year-round flea market.

The hay barn had been thoroughly cleaned and hadn't seen a bale in over a decade, but it still smelled sweet and grassy when I stepped inside. Dust motes drifted lazily in the sunbeams that slanted through the windows, and the elderly gentleman in pressed overalls and a checkered shirt was doing his darnedest to keep his myriad wares fresh and gleaming. A charming if losing battle.

I heard the scuttle of tiny feet and realized he wasn't alone. There was a brownie here, one of the nice fairies. Fairy, not fae. There was a caste system among the Fair Folk: high fae, lesser fae, fairy, and the Big Nasty. Pixies and brownies were fairies, mostly nice and harmless, and eager to be a part of everyday life. Pixies being the mischievous kittens who got into *everything* and brownies the elusive household helpers who took pride in the cleanliness and tidiness of their homes.

Or barns, in this case. But by the looks of it, this indoor flea market needed an entire family of brownies. Maybe even an army.

At the sound of the little bell, the elderly man looked up from polishing the intricacies of a cuckoo clock and adjusted his wire-rim glasses. "Help you, Miss...?"

"Misty," I said firmly, reminding even myself. "Misty Fields." It'd been my favorite sight every morning at the manor; it would be an easy alias to maintain.

His bushy white eyebrows rose into his thick white hair.

"I know, I know." I flashed a self-depreciating smile. "I sound like I should be in a Bond film."

He gave an amused snort and gently set the cuckoo clock aside. "Hollywood would never. They'd be too afraid a country girl like you could out-shoot, out-drive, and out-drink that ol' 007."

As a Hawthorne, I could do a fair more than that—Grand-mother Iris and the rest of the coven had seen to that—but I didn't want to. Ever again.

"The name's Emmett Trinket," the elderly man introduced. "And you must be the one who purchased that old farmhouse on Apple Blossom, yeah? Gonna get that apple orchard and cider press up and running again?"

The farmhouse advertisement had made mention of the adjoining "quaint and rustic" apple orchard and cider press, which was really just code for "decrepit," but I'd yet to lay eyes on it to confirm. I needed the pixies out of my business before I could focus on restoring the orchard.

But I was looking forward to it. Another old, abandoned place to explore, this one to yield the very fruit to make the most delicious pies of all time? Count me in. After I grab my boots and a bottle of Reisling.

Emboldened by the presence of the brownie, I snapped my fingers, conjuring a bloom of green light at their tips. You'd think a witch on the run like me would avoid using her magic, but that would be like telling an eagle not to fly, a fish not to swim, a cricket not to chirp. To deny that part of me, to not use magic, it hurt. Physically, spiritually, mentally, all the -ally's. It simply went against the laws of nature, and I was a law-abiding citizen, for the most part.

But that's why I had the parasite ring. I'd crafted it myself, a band of briar smoothed down so only one side was thorned and digging into the flesh of my finger, the tourmaline stone I'd purchased at a forgettable pawn shop woven into the band and steadily sucking at my reserves—a leaky faucet relentlessly draining a well. So long as it stayed on my finger, no one would know what I was truly capable of. The citizens of Redbud would only know their newest resident was lumped under the umbrella term "green witch," and one of average power at that, and while I was nice, I was entirely forgettable. It would certainly prevent any snooping.

The green light still glowing mutely at my fingertips, I answered, "That's the plan."

"Ah, seems you've got a greener thumb than the previous owners," Emmett said, not at all perturbed at my mild magic show. He even winked.

That was the nice thing about the town of Redbud: supernaturals and mortals coexisted as easy as two peas in a pod. It's why I'd chosen it—I could blend in here with little effort and only a few secrets.

"Well, you'll find a nice mix of folks here," he continued, adjusting his overalls as he squared his shoulders. I wet my lips to keep from smiling—he was proud about his town. "Always willing to lend a hand, whether furred or not, and plenty of festivals!

"If you're not brewing your own caffeine or alcohol, you'll want to go to the Magic Brewery; it says Axel's Towing on the side of his truck, but the man's also a wizard with anything plumbing, mechanical, or electrical; and while Galloway's got good prices"—he dropped his voice to a whisper—"if you want high-quality porterhouses, you'll really want to go to Sanderson's Processing on Route 146. Their smoked jowl bacon? Change your life."

"Well, I'll definitely have to see about that." Leaning forward, I tapped my hands against the counter. "But first, I'm here for the biggest birdhouse you've got."

"Wanna attract some bluebirds for that veggie garden you'll be growing, no doubt." Another wink.

I smiled again, more genuinely this time, but I didn't correct him, either. He didn't need to know about my business with the pixies, specifically why I was so adamant to get them out of the farmhouse. "Something like that."

There was simply no way the two of us could fit the gigantic birdhouse and its attached post inside my sedan, as packed as it was with boxes and bags and the last vestiges of my former life, plus the groceries, potted herbs, and hardware supplies I'd already stuffed into the front passenger seat, so with a bit of finagling, a braided rug, and a length of cord, Emmett helped me secure the birdhouse to the top of the car.

"Just take the turns slow," he cautioned, testing the tension of the cord with a strum of his finger, "but it should hold. And if you run into Ms. Charlotte Harris in town and she pitches a fit about that birdhouse, you tell her from me she had her chance. You can only enter a man's store so many times and hem and haw without someone else finally snatching it up."

"I will," I promised, sliding into the driver's seat. I closed the door with a timid pull, afraid to rattle the birdhouse balanced precariously on the car's roof.

"Oh!" I stuck my head out the window. "Do you know where I could buy some wood?"

"You whittle, Miss Misty?"

"Heh, no. For the fireplace?"

"I figured that orchard of yours would have enough dead-wood in it, considering how poor of a job the Pembertons did of maintaining it." He scratched the white hair on his head. "But you can always run over to Cody's. He's down the road from Flora's. You know where that is?"

I lifted one of the potted herbs I'd purchased not too long ago and gave it a little shake. The thyme branches wiggled. "Sure do. Thanks again, Mr. Trinket."

"Emmett," he corrected, backing away from the car and waving. "Don't be a stranger now, ya hear?"

In a town this small, it wasn't likely. Which was okay, in moderation. Hawthorne Manor had all of the extended family living under one—albeit sprawling—roof, so I was used to being part of a community. Thrived on it, actually. The closer we were, the stronger our magic, even those who weren't the robed elders of the official coven. And Grandmother didn't tolerate any unhelpful behavior, so me and the siblings and cousins had all turned out pretty decent. A few wilder ones persisted, like my brother Marten, but everyone knew to toe the line.

Until I didn't. Me, the favorite, rebelling? Forget the bottle of Reisling, I'd need a whole case to tell that story.

Forcing my expression to smooth, I stuck my hand out the window in farewell, careful not to jostle the bandages. A low but friendly profile. Yep. That was my destiny in this little town. Not too reclusive on my little apple farm, lest I be branded "odd" and become fodder for the gossip mill, and not central to everyday town life, lest anyone discover what I was really up to at the farmhouse.

And that meant evicting the pixies. Tonight.

CHAPTER TWO

"Please don't fall, please don't fall."

The birdhouse wobbled drunkenly into the upper periphery of the windshield. Biting down on my lower lip, I eased the car to a stop in front of the garden gate, the gravel groaning under the tires. But the corded lashing held, and the birdhouse only mildly swayed as I set the parking brake.

"Thank the Green Mother," I sighed, emerging from the car and giving the birdhouse post a pat. I had a lot to do before sundown and purchasing another birdhouse most definitely wasn't on my list of things to do. Once again, I left all my possessions inside the car, removing only the potted herbs and groceries from the front seat. It was time to see how well the crosswinds had worked.

I'd only taken one step over the old threshold when something moved under my foot. "What the—"

In a graceless farce of a pirouette, I spun a haphazard circle. In the same moment I dropped my herbs and groceries, the creeping myrtle flanking the porch suddenly became monstrous vines, catching not only me but the fallen supplies. Periwinkle-blue flowers cushioned apples and the jar of peanut butter as supple tendrils plucked the potted herbs from the air.

The vines righted me into a fighting crouch as I dragged my iron cuffs across each other. The friction illuminated the dormant runes until they blazed like embers, wreathing my wrists in sparking heat. The myrtle vines behind me writhed like the tentacles of a hundred-armed octopus, but there was no danger here. Only a striped marble of white-and-orange glass, which was rattling over the floorboards.

Pain flared in my middle finger, the parasite ring greedily devouring this flare of magic. Between one heartbeat and the next, the myrtle vines were their normal, peaceful selves and my iron cuffs were cool and dormant.

"Heh," I forced out, glancing over my shoulder in the hopes no one had witnessed my, erm, overreaction.

Not a soul.

Thank the Green Mother.

Then I chastised myself for being so easily startled, hissing, "That was stupid, Meadow Hawthorne. If that Vanishing Spell doesn't hold, she can track you by those cuffs." I raised my wrists to eye level, glaring at the woven ivy tendrils of black iron with the Hawthorne berries clasped between the leaves. "Only when your life is at stake."

I'd remove them, if I could, but no doubt that would send up a magical signal flare and then the entire coven would be swooping down on me, Vanishing Spell or not.

My attention shifted to the tourmaline stone of the parasite ring. "And *you*," I said, as if the crystal was sentient, "need to do a better job at keeping my power in check."

It normally didn't glow when it was siphoning off me, but after that recent display, it was like I had an angry firefly trapped in there. Maybe this stone wasn't big enough to keep me in check. Maybe I needed an entire bracelet.

But it'd been doing its job until I freaked out, so maybe it'd be better to investigate what had startled me so badly.

Abandoning the pots and grocery sack, I bent down to retrieve the marble I'd slipped on. The crosswind had probably coaxed it from wherever it'd been hiding. "Don't remember you being here."

That's because it hadn't been there. 1749 Apple Blossom Lane was on the outskirts of town, too remote for youngsters to seek out to play pranks... in theory.

I glanced around outside once more, just to be sure. Only the wind rustled in the nearby maple tree. I'd feel better once I got the hearth fired up. It was a hearth witch's first line of protection and power, after all.

Frowning, I scooped up my supplies and made my way into the kitchen, finding another marble, this one smaller and solid green, right in front of the kitchen sink. Yet another possible twisted ankle in the making. I knew a thing or two about herbal remedies—okay, *a lot*—but twisted ankles took time to heal, or magic, and what I could spare was being diverted to healing my arm. Now that I was alone in an empty farmhouse and not a manor estate with the whole of my extended family, there would be no one to help me if I got hurt. And the three thick rolls of bills I'd removed from the manor safe certainly weren't enough to cover any hospital costs.

With a sigh at the delay, I shoved the groceries into the refrigerator, dug out the dustpan and broom that the Pembertons had clearly forgotten in the nearby coat closet, and searched the house for any more twisted-ankle traps.

I found seven of them.

Seven marbles, all different colors, and all scattered about the house with no rhyme or reason. There were other odds and ends that the puckish wind had released from their hiding spaces: a thimble, a variety of buttons, a few very bright pennies, and three feathers that had to have belonged to a cardinal, a gold finch, and a bluebird at some time. The Pembertons, in addition to leaving behind a neglected orchard, hadn't cleaned up after their grandchildren. It all got swept up, along with all the leaves that had blown into the house, and dumped into the metal trash can outside.

"There." I brushed my hands off then rinsed them under the sink. "No more twisted ankles. Only a mauled arm and a hungry stomach to worry about now."

I had to stop doing that. Talking to myself. It's just that I was so used to a house full of people, of birds twittering in the trees and frogs croaking in the stream, Hawthorne pixies flitting about like dragonflies.

I was so alone here.

My stomach snarled, so I fed it and my emotions with an apple smothered in peanut butter. I would've preferred some of Uncle Stag's triple chocolate bundt cake, because carbs make everything better, but no cake waited under a glass dome on a pedestal on the kitchen counter. I was on my own.

I dug the Dutch oven out of the car along with the rest of my meager kitchen supplies—I'd only managed to grab what had been lying on the trestle table, but what more did a good cook need than a Dutch oven, a big mixing bowl, a wooden spoon, a chef's knife, and a trusty cutting board? *A vegetable peeler.* I riffled through the brown grocery bag to extract just that. *Oh, and a cookie sheet.* Chocolate chip cookies had helped me solve many a problem before, especially when the triple chocolate bundt cake was gone.

For anything else, well, maybe Emmett had such a thing tucked away somewhere in a forgotten corner of his flea market.

Whistling—for it was a natural deterrent for many a mischievous creature—I peeled and chopped onions, carrots, and celery, each addition to the water in the stew pot making homey little *plops* that promised the makings of a flavorful broth. In went a flurry of salt, whole black peppercorns, cloves of garlic, sprigs of thyme, sage, and rosemary, and a few crisp bay leaves. And then, an entire young chicken, which I carefully lowered in by its drumsticks so the boiling broth could flood every crevice instead of overflowing onto the stovetop. It wouldn't be anywhere as good as Aunt Peony's version, but she'd taught me a thing or two when I could be peeled away from Grandmother's elbow.

Turning the flame down, I rubbed my hands with anticipation. It was time for carbs. The white, fluffy kind with a golden crust.

Nothing went better with a bowl of chicken soup than a chunk of homemade bread still steaming hot from the oven. While most green witches and homesteaders swore by sourdough—and it indeed had its merits—I preferred the less tangy variety of artisanal bread. Flour, a little salt, a spoonful of sugar, only a quarter teaspoon of yeast, a flood of warm water and voilà, the perfect loaf. The high moisture content and a day-long rise would create the gluten strands all by itself, no kneading required. Which was just as well, for I still needed to tackle that birdhouse.

With the chicken soup simmering away and the mixing bowl covered by a tea towel and set in the sun to warm, I returned, yet again, to the car. While it had taken the two of us to get it up there on the roof, it would only take one to slide the birdhouse and its post off the front hood in a control descent to the ground. Which was what the braided rug was for: scratch prevention and slide facilitation. It was a worn and faded thing, much like everything else Emmett and his brownie hadn't managed to polish in his flea market, but it was still thick and sturdy and could be repurposed in the front hall once I'd shaken the dust out of it.

Just as I finished tugging free the last length of cord from the birdhouse, the hair on the back of my neck prickled.

Really, they're back already?

I'd learned to trust my instincts from a very young age, for how else could I connect to my magic and the world around me if I wasn't listening and paying attention? And as part of the Hawthorne family, well, if I wasn't watchful there was a sibling or a cousin sneaking buckthorn essence into my afternoon tea, and then it would be endless trips to the bathroom all evening.

I glanced over my shoulder, fast, the brown locks of my ponytail whipping around to lash against my other cheek. You had to be fast to catch sight of pixies, even if you yourself were fae or supe. Naturally I'd assumed the more bold and curious ones would be scurrying from sight, but there was nothing by the garden gate, nor the decrepit flowers, nor at the farmhouse whose doors and windows were still open and releasing the gentle smells of soup and rising dough.

Frowning, I turned back around to the birdhouse, and two yellow eyes stared straight back at me.

I froze, soundless with fear.

There in the gravel driveway, on the opposite side of the car, was a cat.

Now the normal, non-magical individual would've greeted it in one of two ways: an abrasive shout to make it run off, or a silly coo in an attempt to befriend it.

I did neither. I knew, as the much of the magical world did, that a cat was rarely a cat. It could be a shifter, a druid, even a fairy or a Big Nasty cursed to a fleshy prison. Or something glamoured to look like something else, like that not-dog at the manor had been.

We'd had cats in the garden to keep the mice away, but they'd all worn collars of braided gold wire with moonstone nametags. The only way we could be sure that our cats were indeed our *cats*.

This one was what the cat aficionados of the world would call a caliby. White splashed its throat and belly while red-and-brown tabby stripes variegated along its back. Ears pricked forward, it watched me with unblinking yellow eyes.

I swallowed, hands still hovering over the birdhouse. I'd have to put some distance between me and the car if I didn't want the birdhouse to catch fire when I activated my iron cuffs.

No iron cuffs, I reminded myself sharply. But moving away was still a good idea.

That would require a brisk step or jump back, and if this cat was really a Big Nasty wearing a glamour, it would have its jaws around me faster than that.

Maybe I was being paranoid. This was Redbud, Indiana, after all. No one knew I was here. They didn't even know my real name. And I'd been thorough when covering my tracks, both magical and physical. Grandmother and Dad had taught me that, though I was sure they would be kicking themselves for that same fact whenever the Vanishing Spell wore off. If it ever did.

Wetting my lips, I returned the cat's stare for only a moment, belatedly remembering it wasn't the polite thing to do. My gaze drifted, not fully away from the cat, for that would be stupid if it was indeed a Big Nasty or a shifter or druid or any other supe, but just... lower.

And saw an alternative to my iron cuffs. Those nearby morning glory vines choking the front garden fence could lash out and tangle that cat or non-cat right up into a viny cocoon, and *then* I could finish it off with the power of the cuffs. But I'd have to remove the parasite ring first, and that was not in my best interest. But staying alive certainly was, so it was a toss-up. Though, I suppose I could just dash into the kitchen for a handful of salt and my iron chef knife. The homesteader's trusty fae-be-gone.

It only took a moment to decide against all of it. This creature was assessing me like a headmistress would a new pupil, for whatever reason, and if I wanted to forge a new life in Redbud with my little apple orchard, then I'd best give it the benefit of the doubt.

Just to be safe, I slid my ivy-green eyes to the side to view the cat out of my periphery. Fae glamours held really well when seen straight on, but from the side... fuzzy edges revealed an alternative physical reality. This cat, however, did not have any fuzzy edges other than what its fur already provided.

Keeping my magic to myself and the morning glory vines right where they were, I returned my full attention back to the cat and gave it one slow blink. The cat, if it really was a cat, for I still wasn't convinced until it wore a braided golden collar with a moonstone tag, seemed to accept this social nicety and lifted from its seated position without any noise at all. Tail lifted high, it sauntered down the gravel driveway to the road where it turned left towards the forest, away from town, and out of sight.

"Thanks for stopping by," I called, a wary note in my voice. It never hurt to be polite, even if it really was a Big Nasty in cat's clothing. When the cat—or any other nefarious creature—didn't return, I finally relaxed and settled my hands on the birdhouse. "Let's get you sorted, shall we?"

CHAPTER THREE

THE BIRDHOUSE WAS MORE A BIRD HOTEL THAN A HOUSE WITH three tiers and six individual nest boxes on each tier. There was a wraparound porch on the ground tier and little perch posts for tiny feet outside the holes for the rest. An acorn finial capped its peaked roof like a cherry on a chocolate cake, and after a hefty dose of lemon-yellow and rose-pink paints, it looked rather homey.

I'd read a thing or two about pixies, you see, and the scholars all agreed that cheerful paint and a cozy new home were key to evicting pixies. A cotton ball plopped into each nesting box accentuated the coziness and went, I hoped, the extra mile. Wedging the post upright near the house where it could finish drying, I got to work on the garden.

"Well this is a hot mess and no mistake." Yet I sank down to the ground eagerly.

After the days spent in the car driving from the East Coast to this little haven in the middle of the Midwest, I hadn't had much time to connect to the earth. "Green witch" was the catchall term for my kind—hearth, hedge, and forest witches alike, plus a great deal many other subcategories—and we all had to rejuvenate ourselves with nature.

Grounding might be what all the millennials were raving about these days, but it'd been essential to us witches for millennia. I had to touch the earth daily to literally ground both me and my magic. It's why all us youngsters—anyone under thirty, according to my family's definition—ran around the manor barefoot all day every day. The robed elders of the coven wore supple leather boots, but only because they were the face of our family and had to look "presentable" on occasion. Though, Grandmother had told of stories of Violet, said to be the sister of the Green Mother herself, and no one in their right mind would have ever told that witch to comb her hair or clean her feet.

Except for the goldfish sprout I'd spirited away in the cupholder of my car, there hadn't been a speck of greenery to touch as I'd fled inland. There wasn't time to spare, lest my proximity undo the Vanishing Spell I'd cast, and the hotel I'd finally swerved into was just a shabby building on a vacant lot so void of life not even weeds grew in the cracks in the asphalt. I'd held the goldfish plant close that night, cupped in my palms, an irrational fear that it would die there if I didn't shelter it.

And now that it was safe and I had this little fenced-in garden and lawn and an apple orchard, I could finally breathe. Slipping a hand beneath my shirt collar, I withdrew the amazonite pendant Grandmother had given me at my confirmation ceremony all those years ago and let it hang free.

The dirt felt good as I sank my fingers into the ground. Years of composted maple leaves and spent flowers had improved the clay soil to a looser loam that would more readily accept my magic. Green light flowed from my fingertips, sparking gold as it caught on to my relief, and seeped into the ground. I poured out every ounce I hadn't funneled away to treat my arm, nor that which was being siphoned off by the parasite ring. All that green magic I'd stored away in the amazonite pendant bypassed the ring, racing through the earth eagerly.

Some of our family needed stones and crystals as focuses for their magic, their own gift too weak to perform whatever task— for Grandmother forbade the use of familiars—but a handful of us used the crystals as batteries. Extra magic to call upon when needed. Indeed, you had to be such a witch, female or male— not a warlock, mind you, they were a different supe all together, and a nasty one at that—to even be considered for candidacy into the circle of nine. My older brother Marten had become its newest member the same week I ran away with the very thing he was sworn to protect.

My magic wavered with my thoughts, and I could feel it drawing back. Why heal the land when its caster was in need?

Your mind belongs on your task, Grandmother's voice suddenly chastised. *Imagine what you could accomplish if you'd just focus!*

There'd been a reason why Marten had succeeded as the coven's newest member even though he hadn't been the strongest candidate. I was too easily distracted.

A habit I had to break, otherwise my escape from Hawthorne Manor was all for naught.

Shaking the residual echoes of Grandmother's lessons from my head, I concentrated on the ground. My arm wasn't in dire straits anymore. This garden needed more of a healing touch than I did.

The pulsing waves that rippled away from my hands cropped the grass and shriveled the weeds and made whatever flowers that had managed to poke free of the overgrowth flourish with new buds. It shuffled the brick pavers up from their mossy graves and back to the surface, reestablishing the path from the garden gate to the front porch. My magic spread with my smile, all the way to the maple tree at the southern tip of the garden, the leaf-laden limbs seeming to swell with renewed vigor. It rippled across the wildflower fields beyond the fence, but I pulled it back at the edge of the orchard; there would be time to focus on that another day.

It did nothing for the fencing, which needed some new paint, nor the rusty latch on the garden gate, nor the farmhouse, and yet, the place seemed livelier. Renewed. Like a giant had breathed in a great blustering breath of new life into the property. And there was still power left in the pendant. Swallowtail butterflies, which I hadn't seen before, now flitted about the zinnias and cosmos.

My magic had also created a row of mounded dirt along the perimeter of the garden, between the fence and the existing flowers, as well as a hole on the east side, the perfect depth for the birdhouse post. After moistening the bag of cement with water from the garden hose, I poured it into the hole and wrangled the birdhouse post in after it. At my magical request, a few helpful purple clematis vines thickened and wrapped around the post to hold it steady and level. Then I shuffled my feet against the mounded dirt to backfill the hole, stomping to tamp it down.

I brushed the dirt off my palms. "That's not half bad. But it still needs—"

My stomach snarled, demanding sustenance. While I hadn't drained the pendant, I'd drained my reserves and the power it took to direct that much magic. And even though I was soaking up magic from the earth with every step, I needed to refuel in more ways than one.

I could just hear the phantom voice of my Grandmother rising from the recesses of my mind, harping on something related to mindfulness—go figure—and waved it away before it could take root.

My stomach eagerly suggested I check on the stew pot, and my legs just as eagerly abandoned the garden for the kitchen.

The fragrant scent of rich homemade broth enveloped me like a warm hug and set my mouth to salivating. But a full meal would have to wait. It wasn't simply chicken soup boiling away on the stove, but bone broth, and it needed more time.

Slotting the wooden spoon into the chicken's cavity, I lifted the steaming bird from the pot and set it on the cutting board to cool enough so I could debone it. With the meat reserved in a Ziplock bag, filching succulent pieces along the way, I carefully dumped the bones back into the stew pot and let it simmer away. As I packed the bag into the refrigerator for tonight's dinner, I withdrew another apple, slathered it with peanut butter as I was wont to do, and returned to my chores outside.

"Let the pixie-proofing begin," I said aloud. Did it count as talking to myself if the pixies weren't around to listen? I didn't doubt for a moment that a few lurked nearby, watching. Well, it was only fair to give warning, just as I had with the spiders.

At Flora's Garden Dreams, I'd purchased every seed packet of delphinium in the store. Blue, purple, white, pink, I mixed the varieties all together in my palm and sprinkled them along the mounded border of the garden, careful to go around the newly staked birdhouse, and stopped at the garden gate. That's where I'd plant the rosemary and lavender, for protection.

Once the seeds and potted herbs were all watered in well, I dug my fingers into the garden bed once more. My magic reserves had already swelled during my little break in the kitchen—I'd always rejuvenated quickly—and I had plenty from the pendant to build the floral boundary that would keep the pixies from snooping inside my new house.

Delphinium spears rose three feet in height before bursting into bloom, lavender buds popped into tiny purple tongues, and the scent of rosemary became heady and pungent. I steadied myself on my hands and knees for a moment, swaying in place from nearly draining myself twice in one day, and started to chuckle. "It's worth it. No matter how long it takes, they'll see it in the end."

I wasn't talking about the pixies.

With a steeling breath, I heaved myself upright. *First things first and second things second, after all.* Rest, particularly a nap on a sunny patch of lawn, would have to wait until after I finished unloading the car. Wouldn't want the now-evicted pixies taking out their frustrations on my possessions. They'd leave the sedan well enough alone, as it was metal, but if I didn't want my clothes knotted and bits of finery cracked, they had to make it into the house before twilight.

Rooting around in the various boxes and bags crammed in the back seat and trunk, I finally located the box with the linens. I brought that box in first, tossing the gingham picnic blanket over the porch railing as I went inside. It would serve as a constant reminder as I made the multiple trips to and from the car to get my belongings into the house as quick as I could, for sunlit patches of lawn didn't last.

CHAPTER FOUR

THE CORNER OF THE GINGHAM PICNIC BLANKET LIFTED WITH THE breeze in a lazy farewell as the sedan and I trundled back down the gravel drive. While it shouldn't have taken much time to unload the random assortment of bags and boxes from the car —I was just shoving it all into the foyer to unpack and sort later —my steps going and returning down the garden path were slow. There was a finality about all of this I hadn't come to grips with yet.

And this trip into town, to Cody's, would seal it for me. Truly make this my new reality.

I hadn't *left* the manor estate. I'd *fled*. I'd been so blinded by fear and tears and pain and *everything* that I wasn't even sure if the Vanishing Spell I'd cast had taken proper root. Someone as powerful as Grandmother could have nullified it and set the coven—my family—after me.

They couldn't find me. Not until my work in Redbud was done.

When my fingers started trembling on the steering wheel, I forced them to tighten and blinked my ivy-green eyes clear. Hawthorne eyes. That's who I was, even if I was going by the surname Fields, and the most powerful witch of my generation. I could survive this.

I pulled the amazonite pendant free of my shirt and rubbed it with my thumb, finding comfort with the familiar movement.

The little town of Redbud was becoming as familiar as my pendant in the short amount of time I'd already spent there. Every road seemed to lead to one of the four spokes of the town center's rotary, and from that compass center it was pretty easy to determine which way you needed to go. My farmhouse and the small diner Patty's were on the east side of the rotary, Galloway's to the north, Emmett's Barn Market and Hammer & Nails to the west, and Flora's Garden Dream to the south. And Cody's.

Emmett hadn't given me any more specifics than that, and I hadn't thought to ask. From the familiar way he spoke of it, Cody's had to be pretty recognizable. And it was.

A barn large enough to rival Emmett's squatted close to the road, a wide dirt parking lot large enough for two logging trucks to park in parallel right beside it. The barn was painted forest green with black trim, the emblem of a wooden bench between two pine trees painted in ivory above the massive double doors. They were open, revealing not the insides of a barn at all, but a carpenter's workshop.

I parked on the far-right side beside the Cedar Haven truck, careful to leave enough space in the lot for any deliveries that might show up during my visit. A forest encroached on the entire establishment, looming in as if at any moment it would reclaim the felled trees stacked off to the side of the barn. Piles of mulch in two different colors, red and blond, squatted beside the logs, each as almost as tall as hay bales.

Sliding out the car, I shut the door with a gentle click lest it echo like a gunshot in this quiet place. My eyelids fluttered shut as my lungs expanded with a deep, instinctual breath, and I listened.

There was a saw mill at the bottom of the nearby slope, dormant, even its river somehow muted, and the carpentry machines inside the barn were silent. A serenity that only the wild places of the world could provide radiated from the forest. It was old and full of secrets, just like the one that edged the manor. Though I doubted the fabled Stag Man that Grandmother had frightened us with could be found here.

Another deep breath, and my eyes opened.

Across from where I'd parked, a little worn path wound away into the forest, sunlight illuminating a clearing with a little sod-roofed cottage and a nearby stream that must feed into the river. Smoke coiled in a languid gray thread from the stone chimney; a motorcycle glinted in the sunlight beside a brick-edged flowerbed. And was that the droning of beehives I heard?

I slipped the pendant back under my collar and was halfway through loosening the ties of my gypsy shirt when my fingers stilled. What was I doing? Just because this place was wilder than anywhere else I'd yet seen in town didn't mean I couldn't strip down to my undies and frolic with wild abandon, no matter what my magic was insisting on! I wasn't back at the manor under the moon of the vernal equinox; there were people here! Though I'd yet to see them yet.

So with my clothes and shoes still firmly on my body, I marched across the parking lot, pausing at the open doors of the workshop to call, "Hello? Is anyone there?" I stuck my head inside, squinting into the gloom and dust motes that smelled like cedar. "Hello?"

"Can I help you?" a deep voice asked from behind me.

Thistle thorns! I hadn't even heard him approach!

I whirled with a yelp, magic flaring to my fingertips. Not the emerald green color of my morning's work, but darker, like the needles of the surrounding pines or of ivy when it's been growing in shade instead of sunlight. The kind that fueled my iron cuffs.

You're in Redbud, Meadow, the literal middle of nowhere! They probably don't even know what Big Nasties are. I quickly snuffed it out, the parasite ring guzzling greedily, and remembered my manners. Then immediately wondered if that had been a mistake.

The man standing before me was definitely *other*, just like I was. Broad shoulders weren't so much hidden under red plaid flannel and suspenders as they were accentuated, fine dark brown hair wisping out from the *V* left behind from the undone buttons at his throat. Sweat glittered there and across his forehead, though it could've been spray from the river. He'd come up from there on the sawmill path, a log as thick around as my waist poised over one shoulder. Flecks of wood shavings speckled his dark brown hair and beard. He was powerfully built, an intensity roiling off of him like heat radiating from pavement on a summertime day.

Change that lumberjack outfit for motorcycle leathers and you had yourself a Grade A Bad Boy.

By the Green Mother, what was a man like *that* doing hidden away in sleepy ol' Redbud? How in the world was I going to keep a low and friendly profile knowing *he* was running around town? I wasn't a liberated woman like Cousin Lilac—Aunt Hyacinth called her "the Destroyer of Manly Hearts, Souls, and Loins"—but I had eyes. And thoughts. Which had no place in my head when I was here in Redbud for one reason and one reason only.

I backed away from him with a loud gulp, heart pounding. Everything about him was magnetic from his sheer physical presence to that glimmer in his gentle hazel eyes. So maybe less

Bad Boy and more Gentle Giant than I'd originally thought. Either way... *Thistle thorns, I'm in trouble.*

He seemed just as surprised by me as I was of him, or maybe he was just perplexed that a strange woman had screamed when all he'd done was offer her help. Regardless, he recovered first by quipping, "Trouble?" Though his brow crinkled in question, his eyes twinkled.

By the Green Mother, please *tell me I didn't just say that out loud!* "Uhh..."

I cleared my throat and reined in my thoughts. He was *other*, which meant supe or fae. A quick sideways glance revealed no fuzzy edges, so he wasn't glamoured.

A shifter, then. Or maybe a druid or mage, but you didn't see many of them hauling tree trunks like they were sacks of grain. Definitely a shifter. And definitely forbidden. Grandmother had been very clear about that, just as she had about exploring the forest around the manor: *Not. Ever.*

That divine gift to the gene pool of a man who was definitely a shifter heaved the log onto the stack of felled trees, brushed the debris from his shirt, and asked again in the same gentle tone as before, "Can I help you, Miss...?"

"Mea—Misty," I caught myself. Thistle thorns, he must have my head spinning if I'd been about to give him my real name. I swallowed hard, finding it very difficult indeed to break my attention from those hazel eyes. But I did. Fixed them right on his boots like a good girl. "M-my name's Misty. Misty Fields."

"Arthur Greenwood."

I risked an upwards glance, confused. Bad idea. Those hazel eyes had me again. "But Emmett said this was Cody's place?"

"It is Cody's. I just work for him. Excuse me." He passed by to duck inside the workshop, returning with a water canteen and a plastic container of peanut butter crackers. Homemade. With honey sandwiched with the peanut butter, if my nose wasn't mistaken.

When he offered me some, it took every ounce of willpower to resist. They smelled delicious, and I was always starving after expending my magic, but taking him up on his offer would require I come closer. And getting closer to that man was definitely a bad—and yet perfectly wonderful—idea.

"You don't look like Cody, though, right?" I didn't know why I asked that, probably to make sure there wasn't another one just like him that I'd have to worry about. One distraction was obviously enough. "He's not your twin brother or anything?"

Arthur threw his head back with a laugh. "You must be new in town."

"Why are you laughing?" a new voice said, coming up the same sawmill path. "You wish you looked this good."

A steel-haired man dressed identically as Arthur yet as old as Emmett wheezed as he crested the slope, dropping a wicker basket full of paper birch bark on the pine needles at his feet. Where Emmett had a bit of a paunch due to his sedentary life on his stool polishing knickknacks, this man was as lean as a sapling, his clothes drooping off hanger-like shoulders.

Removing his ball cap, which was embroidered with the same bench-and-pines logo on the barn, he slicked back his steel hair with a sigh. He then stretched, his spine popping. "And you were new in town once, too, boy, don't forget. Wasn't that long ago neither."

"Let me help you with that," I said, rushing forward for the basket. Old Uncle Hare had the same propensity for overworking himself, his wiry body still hale but without the strength of his youth. Looked like him, too.

"I got it, miss." Arthur stepped in front of me, my view suddenly blocked by a wall of red plaid, suspenders, and chest.

The heady scent of fresh-cut pine and old-growth forest immediately flooded the air between us.

A glint of yellow and a flash of iridescent wings broke through the momentary sensory overload, and I lurched forward, hand raised. "Don't move! You've got a—"

Arthur caught my hand before I could touch him, callouses grating against my softer skin.

"—bee!" I finished, straining a finger forward to point. "Right there, on the collar of your shirt."

Without releasing me, he shifted his hazel gaze down to the fold in red plaid. "Huh. So I do. Must be Pansy or Yarrow."

"Wh-what?" *He's named the bees?*

He offered a finger to the honeybee, who buzzed onto his fingernail. Arthur lifted the bee to eye level. "Pansy likes to visit from time to time, but, ah, this is Yarrow. The freeloader. Don't you have work to do?"

He blew gently, the bee flying away on his breath. Then he shifted his gaze back to me, all trace of his former gentleness gone.

Tension thrummed through me in response, the darker magic rising, but I kept in check. That's not who I wanted to be.

"I'm a logger *and* a beekeeper," he said sternly, "so I'd appreciate it if you didn't squash my bees."

I tried to tug my hand free, but his grip only hardened. Amber flashed in those hazel eyes. Most definitely a shifter, though I still didn't know what kind. Didn't matter to a Hawthorne, especially not one like me. Though, that parasite ring... it definitely put us on a level playing field.

"I wasn't going to squash her," I said, keeping my tone level. "I was simply going to brush her away. If she stung you, she would've lost her stinger and died. I was trying to help—didn't know if you were allergic or anything."

His eyes widened at the same time his grip slackened. "I'm sorry," he blurted.

I pulled free and backed up another step, flattening my arm across my stomach. He'd had one powerful grip, one that had stressed the healing wounds along my arm.

"Arthur, you foolish boy, you've scared her," Cody chastised.

"I'm not scared," I said quickly. Hotly. It took much more than a man, even a supe as big as him, to scare a Hawthorne.

Though I'd spent more time in the fields and flowers than my family, I still hadn't missed one combat training session. While some families performed yoga at dawn, we tried to break each other with magic or our fists.

"Yeah," Arthur said, giving me wink. It was an apology and a compliment all in one. "Country girls don't scare easy, anyway. Now move over, old man." Sputtering, Cody side-stepped as the big lumberjack shifter muscled into his space. He hefted the basket as if it weighed nothing at all and carried it into the workshop. "And this is heavier than you should be lifting."

"Last time I checked you worked for me, not the other way around, so show some respect," he barked, but there was no bite to it. Only a grin for me. "Cody Beecham," he finally introduced, "pleased to meet you, Miss...?"

"Misty Fields."

"So, what's brought you around to the Cedar Haven? Need a porch swing? Wardrobe? Custom bar stools? Something smaller like hand-carved kitchen utensils or salt cellars?"

"I'm just here for ash wood, if you have it. Or rowan. Maybe holly?"

"That's... specific. Do you mind if I ask what you're needing it for?"

There was nothing *other* about him, but I still wanted to keep my business exactly that—my own. It was the whole reason I was evicting the pixies after all, plus they could be worse than termites. "Why do you need to know?" I asked lightly.

"No offense meant. It's just the woods you're requesting aren't your typical firewood, so they're not sourced in abundance. Holly is usually just an ornamental, so you'd have to see Flora about that, and these forests don't have any rowan. What ash I have is quality grade, meant for decorative furnishings. It's quite pricey."

I chewed my bottom lip as I did some internal calculations. "I don't need much. And it can be just shavings or off-cuts or—"

Cody snapped his twig-like fingers. "You know what? I have this rather knotty piece I can't seem to find any use for. It's just been sitting in my scrap pile, waiting for inspiration, or you, it seems. I'll sell it to you half off, sound fair?"

I stuck out my hand. "It's a deal."

"Fantastic." He shook it then hooked his thumbs in his suspenders. "Now, you sure I can't get you anything else while you're here? No Adirondack chairs or woodland figurines for your front garden? What about a basket? I weave a mean basket. Literally. Some are studded with porcupine quills. Perhaps a bench for a secluded lover's nook?" He waggled his eyebrows. He mercifully didn't look to where Arthur had disappeared into the workshop.

"Now who's scaring her?"

That rumbling voice preceded the shifter like thunder before a storm, Arthur returning with another water canteen and a small amber jar. He handed the bottle to Cody and offered me the jar. "For your arm, miss."

"My arm?" It was still snuggled against my stomach.

"Your wound."

Instead of looking down, I searched his face. How'd he known that? My wounds were sealed. Raw, sure, but sealed and on the mend, thanks to my magic. And he'd only touched my hand, not the bandage-wrapped forearm, which was pretty undiscernible beneath the billowing sleeves of my gypsy shirt. Maybe he wasn't a shifter at all. Maybe he was one of those mystical healing druids who just bench-pressed a lot? "How did you...?"

He pointed to a dot of red on my sleeve. Literally no larger than a seed. "I tend bees, miss. I'm used to noticing little things."

Ah, so still a shifter. Noticed a speck of blood that had been hidden in the fold of my sleeve? Yeah, noticed it with his *nose*, not his eyes.

"Oh, um, thanks." To take the topic off my arm, and what else he'd gleaned, I unscrewed the jar and gave it a sniff. "What's this?"

"Calendula extract mixed with honey and some beeswax. It's—"

"Antimicrobial, antibacterial, anti-inflammatory, and speeds up healing, especially skin wounds. Thanks!"

Arthur's hazel eyes widened once more, mouth dropping open. "Yeah. Exactly."

"Your mouth's still open," Cody snickered, taking a sip of his water.

Arthur cleared his throat and indicated my sedan with a jerk of his bearded chin. "Not sure the ash knot can fit in there. It's more like a stump than a log. Might need to trailer it over."

"No, no," I said quickly. The fewer visitors I had to the farmhouse, the better. Especially since the wards weren't up yet. I flashed a smile to assuage their suspicions. "Can you just bring it out here? I'll make it fit."

He ran a hand through his dark brown hair and glanced at Cody. "Okay."

A moment later, the muscles in his arms fit to bursting, the lumberjack shifter strode out of the workroom with not just a stump, but an entire root ball of an ash tree in his grip.

Cody chuckled at my look of dismay and said, "I'll pull around the truck."

"No need, gentlemen," I declared, striding over to pop the trunk. They'd been calling me "miss" and pussyfooting around with their politeness like I was someone with tender sensibilities. "Though, might I bother you to borrow a tarp or something?"

"I'll go get a tarp," Cody said, changing direction.

Arthur carried the massive piece of wood over to the car, pausing in some sort of half-squat where he leaned back as a counterweight to the stump that rested on bulging thighs. "I'm only lifting and putting this thing down once," he said stiffly.

Cody and I lined the trunk bed with the old tarp, then I tapped my thumb against my bottom lip as I assessed the stump. Or rather, how Arthur was keeping both him and it upright. *Cousin Boar, I think I just found a challenger for your longest weighted horse stance record.*

"It's not getting any lighter," Arthur grunted.

"I'm sure it's not," I mused. "But this is payback for being all rude and handsy about the bee."

"That's what the apology and the salve were for!"

"Well, I had to be sure."

Old man Cody guffawed.

"And you can put it down now," I said.

"But," he protested.

"Quit showing off and set the stump down," Cody said, smacking Arthur in the arm. The old man shook out bruised fingers. "Ack! You're supposed to be helping me, boy, not getting a workplace injury that drains my insurance *and* leaves me without an assistant!"

The ash stump landed in the dirt with a crack. Panting slightly, Arthur crossed his arms over his chest and lifted a dark eyebrow. "Well? How is *that* going to fit in *there*?"

Smirking, I snapped my fingers, conjuring emerald green light. This was simple magic, and low expenditure, so the parasite ring remained dormant. Cody guffawed again, shoving an immovable Arthur, and the lumberjack shifter just groaned, rolling his eyes. With just a touch of my magic-laced fingers, I split the stump into eight manageable portions and cleaved off the odd-shaped roots that would hinder stacking the wood in my trunk.

Placing another glowing finger against the ground, I gave life to the seeds hidden in the dirt, and, thanks to the parasite ring, only one thick vine sprouted free at my call. One proved enough. It coiled around the closest piece of wood and lifted it into the trunk. Cody broke out into a deep belly laugh that arched his back enough that he threatened to snap his own spine. But his mirth wasn't for me. It was directed at his brawny assistant, whose face was still red from manhandling the stump.

As Cody laughed, Arthur endured, and I leaned against the car watching them with a smug lift to my lips, the tentacle-like vine carefully fitted every piece of ash wood into place, even closing the trunk door with a decisive slam before slithering back into the dirt and disappearing.

"Thank you, gentlemen," I said, straightening and flicking my brown ponytail over my shoulder. I opened my purse to pay for the wood.

"You're a green witch," Arthur accused. For a moment, I wondered if his own grandmother had warned him away from my kind as my grandmother had me of his, but his voice could only be described as amused incredulity. "You could've said something."

I didn't correct him. Hawthornes were renowned *hearth* witches, but Misty Fields was just your average green witch.

"And miss the show?" I asked innocently instead, handing Cody a stack of bills.

"No, no," the old man said, waving his hands. "That's too much. Half that."

I counted it again. "But you said—"

"That was the price before you gave my boy a run for his money. *I'm* paying *you* for that pleasure."

Arthur gave the old man a narrow look. "Has anyone ever told you you're a horrible boss?"

"If they have, they certainly don't work for me anymore. Remember that." He touched his fingers to the brim of his ball cap. "Have a good day, Misty Fields. A pleasure meeting you, but these old bones need a sit."

He left me and the lumberjack shifter just staring at each other. My impertinent bravery suddenly vanished as he took a step forward, full lips parting to say—

"Well, um, thanks for the wood. And the salve," I said, spinning around to yank open the car door. Shifters were forbidden for a reason, and if they were all like this with their magnetism and fantasy-inducing thoughts, as my mind was currently well on its way of doing, I had to avoid Arthur Greenwood like the plague. "And sorry for my part in the misunderstanding about the bee."

That snowshoe of a hand curled around the door frame, pulling it open further so I wouldn't have to do some sort of slithering shimmy into the seat. I turned, my pulse jumping as the gentleness returned to his hazel eyes.

"Let me know if you need anything else, miss."

By the Green Mother, had his voice dropped another octave or was my brain short-circuiting? *Trouble*, I reminded myself. *Say it with me, Meadow. TROUBLE.* Thistle thorns, where was Cousin Lilac when I needed her? She'd think of something smart to say and not look stupid doing it either. "O-okay."

Smooth. Real smooth.

"Sometimes it's good to know a guy with a truck and a trailer," he continued, yet to release the door. If anything, he was closer. Oh my Green Mother, I never knew I would be so attracted to the smell of old-growth forest. "You can call the shop, though we sometimes can't hear it, or text..."

He dug around in his back pocket and pulled out a business card. Flipping it over, he had to release the door to scrawl a number across the back.

Huh. The area code was different. "Yours?" I asked.

Arthur dragged a hand through his thick brown hair, releasing another sprinkling of wood shavings. That scent of fresh-cut pine and old-growth forest was even heavier now. "Y-yeah. The old man doesn't do much texting; his eyes aren't what they used to be."

"But his ears work just fine!" Cody hollered from the workshop. "Stop flirting. I need your muscles to lift something!"

Flushing red, Arthur ducked his head and bid me a hasty farewell before breaking into a jog.

I wrenched my gaze from where it'd drifted and practically threw myself into the car. The tires squealed—only a little—as I got back on the country road and headed for home. I wasn't driving for more than a handful of seconds before I pinned that business card between my thumb and the steering wheel.

"You idiot," I admonished myself. "I said low and friendly profile, not low and flirty!"

It'd be easy to chuck that business card with Arthur the definitely a shifter's number right out the window, but that would be littering and I couldn't abide by that. So I stuck it between the passenger seat cushions. It was out of sight, out of mind, but if push came to shove and I really needed a guy with a truck and a trailer—and that's *all*—that number would be there, waiting for me.

CHAPTER FIVE

AT THE FARMHOUSE, THERE WAS NO SIGN OF THE CAT FROM earlier that morning and no witnesses to see my graceless, sweaty manhandling of the ash wood logs through the back door and into the hearth room. My magic was suffering from overuse, so I needed to rely on my other strengths. Literally. Since I hadn't sparred with my family in days, the physicality was both needed and appreciated. And the hearth was in desperate need of a fire, so it was all rather fortuitous.

The Hawthornes were hearth witches, their magic strongest when used in the kitchen or at the hearth mixing and bottling potions and tinctures and all manner of elixirs. We also made a really mean tea blend. And unlike other green witches, a hearth witch's magic grew stronger every day her hearth was kept continuously lit.

At the manor, it had been the children who'd been in charge of feeding the hearth fire, though they'd always been overseen by an older relative, though never a robed elder. The robed elders of the coven would never let such an important task be left solely to those distracted by butterflies and the call of song-birds and sunlight. But many young hands made the task of shuttling wood from the giant stack outside to the hearth that much more efficient.

Here, at the farmhouse, it would just be me. I would have to stay vigilant. *Focused*, as Grandmother would say. "No thinking about boys," Aunt Hyacinth had told us girls countless times, though she was really talking to her niece, Cousin Lilac.

Or sexy lumberjack shifters.

The hearth hadn't been used in a very long time, not even during the tenure of the Pembertons, but only the dust of disuse covered the bricks and grate. I heaved the biggest piece of the ash wood onto the grate, topped it with a collection of smaller twigs and branches I'd collected from under the maple tree, and struck a match.

When the flame flared, I whispered, "Smoke of ash, the Mother's bones, form protection 'round this home."

I'd complete the full spell later when the pixies were settled in their new home, but this would suffice for the next few days. Activate the full power of the Hearth Protection Spell now, and those poor creatures were guaranteed a painful death if they came inside uninvited.

I dropped the flame onto the tinder, and a massive green flame engulfed the log. A second passed, the color softening to a natural yellow laced with orange, and heat soon bloomed across the hearth.

The enchantment served two purposes, one which was obvious by the verse, and the other to slow down the fire. It would only consume a fraction of the wood that a normal fire would—unless I had some powerful magic to do—a perk granted to a hearth witch. We didn't want to add any more greenhouse gases to the atmosphere than entirely necessary.

So with that extra time granted, I first checked on the bone broth—still simmering away—then whisked myself out the front door to retrieve the gingham picnic blanket. It was time for a rejuvenating nap in the sun.

And yet after I spread the blanket down on the warm grass, I paused, noticing that more specks of red had joined the first on my sleeve. Moving the logs had obviously agitated the wounds. Retrieving the salve from my purse, I balanced it on my crossed knee as I rolled back the sleeve and uncoiled the bandages.

Almost three full days had passed since that Big Nasty glamoured to look like a dog had attacked me in the manor. I knew better than to say what it was aloud. Even think it. It was too dangerous. Too painful. Too appalling to know my own family had—

"That's not half bad," I forced out instead. The tremor in my voice as I examined the claw marks raking from elbow to wrist said I needed to do a better job at convincing myself. "Not half bad at all. Some of Lumberjack's salve and a sunbathing session or two will cure it right up." And it really would, given a few days. Faster, if I diverted more magic to healing it.

But I might need it for something else.

A little surprised gasp escaped me when the salve touched my tender flesh. Arthur had added a touch of peppermint to the mix too, the cooling sensation of menthol its own balm to my inflamed skin. What kind of shifter knew herbology, even one who lived in the woods? And what kind of shifter would work for an old man who clearly didn't have a drop of supe blood in him? Certainly not a wolf, they always ran in packs.

Unless he's a lone wolf.

But wolf shifters were typically more aggressive, not the kind to gently lift honeybees from shirt collars.

A dragon, perhaps? They were too vain. Too proud to live in the woods. Maybe he was something more rare, like a bobcat or fox shifter or maybe—I giggled—a *badger*? Ooo, maybe he was the Stag Man Grandmother had warned us about. Nah, he wasn't stately enough for that. What about a bear? Bears liked honey, but they were often more vicious than wolves. At least the wild ones were.

A tingle of excitement raced down my spine and pooled in my belly. Cousin Lilac had dated a shifter once—totally secret, of course—and the stories she'd tell me once we were alone by the hearth sneaking sips of elderberry wine... *By the Green Mother, I hope he's a bear.*

I shook the thought from my head almost as quickly as I'd thought it. It wasn't like I was going to see him again. At least deliberately. Though, small towns had a way of bringing people together.

"You have one job here in Redbud," I told myself sternly. *See, Grandmother? I can focus.* "One job. And that doesn't include swooning over the local hottie. Sure, you might see him again, but you're not *actively* seeking him out. There. Low but friendly profile."

I smeared some more salve onto my wounds, flopped onto my back, and let the warm sunlight lull me into sleep. I hadn't slept well since the night before I'd left the cottage and exhaustion was tugging at me. The sunlight promised easy dreams.

Maybe a bear will be there too...

CHAPTER SIX

Hissing startled me awake.

I was cool, too, for the sunlight that had once bathed me in a warm, end-of-summer glow had indeed moved on. But I didn't jerk upright from my afternoon sprawl. Quick movements startled anything from fae to wild animals to even humans, and it was better to just listen for a moment to discern the danger, if there really was any at all. As I listened, I slunk my hands closer as if to fold them over my stomach. In truth it was just to get my iron cuffs within striking distance.

Only if you have to, I reminded myself. By the Green Mother, what other green witch, subcategory aside, had been trained since infancy to fight? The more I grounded myself out here in the countryside of Redbud, Indiana, the more I began to question my upbringing.

Tsst, tsst, tsst.

The cat or not-cat hadn't returned; the hissing was coming from the stove.

"The bone broth!" Lurching upright, I ran barefoot across the lawn. The screen door to the kitchen slapped against the siding as I plunged inside, yanking the lid back from the stew pot.

"Thank the Green Mother." The bone broth bubbled away, unburnt. The hissing was only the condensation dripping from the slanted lid and onto the hot stovetop. *Thistle thorns, I must be on edge if a few hissing drops have me going for my iron cuffs.*

You know what I like to do when I'm uptight? Cousin Lilac's phantom voice asked.

"Shush, Destroyer of Loins or whatever." I lowered the flame on the stove even more, so it was barely a whisper of blue, and retrieved my wooden spoon for a taste.

The amber-colored broth was luscious and coated my tongue like liquid velvet. That would be the collagen and marrow nutrients, which would lend a luster to my own skin and tempt the favor of the pixies.

Who would be returning any moment, if that sliver of the sun on the western side of the orchard had anything to say about it.

Squinting against direct light of the sunset, I lifted a hand to shade my eyes. While I'd gotten to know the farmhouse and its fenced-in yard pretty well today, I hadn't yet explored the wildflower fields separating the house from the orchard, nor the orchard itself and its buildings, but I could've sworn those three lumps by the orchard fence weren't there before. This far away, they looked like beehives or straw bales slumped against the split rails. Well, from what I'd gleaned from Emmett earlier today, it seemed the orchard was in a bit of disrepair, so that could just be abandoned supplies or whatever.

Abandoning the picnic blanket to pick up at a later time, I climbed the back porch steps and turned around, shading my eyes again and seeing nothing. Huh. Maybe they were just deer passing through. Or woodchucks. That was more likely. This country was wild enough for all sorts of creatures to meander through my new home until I got the hearth running at maximum.

Retreating to the foyer, I set about digging through the various unlabeled boxes and bags I'd dumped there earlier. I'd used a shortcut to pack, a spell Cousin Rose had given me long ago called the Camping Spell. It gathered everything the caster might need for a week-long stay in the woods, but I'd never used it before. Others had always packed for the festivals and family retreats, and I'd always been at Grandmother's elbow mixing and packaging all the remedies we'd need for when someone stumbled into poison ivy in the dark or misidentified a mushroom.

Clothing was packed with bed linens, cutlery with toiletries, and the suspicion that Cousin Rose had been playing a joke on me was confirmed when I withdrew a gravy boat from a box filled with sacks of dried beans and tins of espresso and cartons of matches. Who needed a gravy boat when they went camping?

And yet, it would be perfect.

I continued to root around, just in case, and changed my mind from the spell being a joke to just being a little eccentric. The Camping Spell had packed spare guitar picks—those had to be for Cousin Otter—paracord for all your bondage needs, a supersized bottle of hand sanitizer, a box of bandages, activated charcoal for anyone who ate something they shouldn't have, in addition to an assortment of crockery and cutlery, though none of them matched.

As I heaped an armload of plates, cups, bowls, and utensils into the sink, I let out a shriek. "You again!"

The white, seven-legged garden spider hadn't vacated the premises with its brethren, rather claiming a broad expanse across my kitchen window with its haphazard web. It drew its seven legs under its body in a hunch at the sound of my voice, clearly expecting the swat of a broom to come next. Well, the broom was back in the coat closet, and I wouldn't have used it anyway.

I shook my finger at the spider. "I thought I'd made myself very clear. If I bend over this sink to wash these dishes, I'm going to face-plant into your web. You don't want that, and I most certainly don't, so what'll it be? You need a helping hand out to the garden?"

The spider relaxed and seemed to look down at the goldfish plant.

"Yes, I know it's a pretty flower, but..." My voice trailed off as my gaze shifted from the orange flowers to the web. It was disjointed, fragmented, with little of the symmetry seen in the webs of others of its kind.

"Hard to weave a good net with only seven legs, isn't it?"

The spider had stayed because the goldfish plant would attract insects with its nectar, though most would probably zip right through the large holes in the web. But still, the chance that some would stick would be higher. And if the kitchen window was propped open, then there would be many insect visitors coming to inspect whatever was cooking on the stove. More chances at prey. More chances at life.

"You're lucky you're not a snake," I told the spider. Then I pointed to the upper lefthand corner of the window. "One night, then you're up there, out of the way. You'll still have plenty of bugs, and far more if I'm not wrecking your web with my hair."

The spider spread its legs even more, further relaxing.

"I hope that means you're in agreement, otherwise I'm tossing you outside." Then, with much more care than I normally put into washing dishes, I prepped for the pixies' inevitable return.

Though I wouldn't necessarily see them, there would be signs. A gentle buzzing like that of hummingbirds' wings, the faint scent of goldenrod, and a sharp tug on my brown ponytails if they were feeling particularly puckish—if they could get through the floral wards, which they couldn't. In theory. I was assuming Midwest pixies were like East Coast pixies and could be easily bribed away to a new home. The books I'd read on the subject hadn't mentioned any regional differences.

The gravy boat would be the perfect trough in which to feed them; I simply did not have enough thimbles—minus the one I'd found in the middle of the master bedroom that was now in the outdoor trash can—to act as pixie-sized soup bowls, and it was too late to return to Emmett's flea market to root through his sewing section to see if he had any. And it wasn't like these were the bougie pixies of the city; I was sure they'd appreciate the spirit of the gesture.

With the dishes drying, I preheated the oven and returned to the bread dough. It slopped out onto the floured counter and didn't resist as I stretched out the sticky corners, folding them back in on themselves until it all resembled a loaf. Uncle Stag was always better at this than me, so I called upon whatever bread-baking spirits he served and hastily transferred the loaf to the cookie sheet—*without* it losing its shape, ha-cha!—and slid it into the oven.

It didn't take long for the kitchen to smell even more glorious than before.

My mouth watering again, I returned to prepping the soup. After straining out all the bits, more fresh carrots and celery were added to the soup and the flame cranked to bring it up to simmer. I went to the refrigerator to retrieve the chicken, and when I shut the refrigerator door, two yellow eyes stared out of the darkening front doorway.

As easily startled as ever, I yelped, though it was more out of surprise than fear. My habit had driven my brother Marten crazy, always rushing from wherever he'd been at my shriek only to find me trapping a mouse or a grass snake—the only serpent I tolerated—under a colander to release it outside.

It wasn't a Big Nasty—their eyes glowed—but I chastised myself all the same for leaving all the doors and windows open. It was great for clearing out pixies, but not preventing whatever *this* was from entering my house.

Except it wasn't *in* my house. The caliby cat was perched on the threshold, and not a toe over it. It lifted its head, nose and whiskers twitching. It clearly smelled the bone broth and the baking bread, and no doubt the chicken in the Ziploc bag in my hands.

"You don't look underfed, but..." It never hurt to be polite. But not too polite. Cats were just as prone to snooping in places they didn't belong as pixies.

I slid the bag onto the counter and pulled out a sliver of dark meat. Then I made a shooing motion with my other hand. "On the porch, kitty cat." I knew better than to invite it inside. The rules that governed vampires on domicile etiquette extended to more than one magical creature. And beasts in general. Give them a taste of indoor life and good luck keeping them outside thereafter.

The cat seemed mildly insulted but backed away as I approached. It didn't flee, head and tail still lifted high as it scented the meat in my hand. But there as a little fine print to my generosity.

"You seem to be a bit of a wanderer," I said. "See anything strange by the orchard fence closest to the house? Three deer, maybe? Woodchucks?"

The cat only flicked its tail.

"Nothing?" I pressed, like I expected it to answer me. Aunt Peony had told me familiars could talk, though only to their bonded witch. "Blink once if no, twice if yes." Blinking was technically not talking.

The cat didn't even twitch a whisker.

Well, that settled... nothing, but I had more important things to do then talk with a cat who didn't talk back. I tossed the chicken towards the steps and quickly shut the door, raising on tiptoe to peek through the door window to see what the cat or not-cat would do.

It had the most judgmental look on its face as it stared right back at me, as if it had known all along that I was going to peer through the door window. It made sure I knew I was judged, then flicked its tail, and sauntered over to the meat.

"You're welcome," I muttered, returning to the stove.

CHAPTER SEVEN

I SLIPPED THE CHICKEN BACK INTO THE BONE BROTH JUST BEFORE taking the bread out of the oven, letting it warm through as the bread cooled. It was nearing twilight now, and if the pixies weren't back already, they would be at moonrise. It was hard to tell what kind of pixie they were without actually seeing them, so I just had to hedge my bets and prepare for all scenarios.

As the smell of fresh bread permeated the kitchen, I ignored my own growling stomach—*again*—and spooned out bone broth into the gravy boat. Just the broth, of course, since pixies preferred bone to flesh. "Bone" being the loosest of definitions to describe their diet. It was the *bones* of anything: buildings (hence the decrepit state of the farmhouse), animals (the bone broth), plants (especially trees and woody stalks, but not the flowers or leaves).

Peeking out the front door for any signs of the cat, I claimed the coast was clear and padded barefoot down the steps with the gravy boat in hand. Swinging to the east, I examined the birdhouse for any signs of life, and, finding none, carefully placed the gravy boat of bone broth on the birdhouse porch facing away from the farmhouse. It was the direction from which they'd most likely come, and maybe they'd be in a more amiable mood if they saw the food offering first thing. With one last glance over my shoulder, I hurried inside for my own dinner. *Finally*.

The soup was delicious, as expected, and I used a bit of warm bread to sop up every last drop of succulent broth. It made the cleanup even easier, leaving plenty of time to start unboxing the rest of my meager belongings.

A variety of sundresses and loose, billowing clothes got hung up on a makeshift clothesline in the kitchen in the hopes that the heat and humidity of the hearth might smooth out the worst of the wrinkles; toiletries and linens found their respective homes in the upstairs bathroom, where the previous owners had left a pink bar of rose-scented soap on the ledge of the clawfoot tub; the tinned groceries and random dry goods were stored away in the kitchen cupboards; the other odds and ends like the matches and hand sanitizer and paracord went into one big designated junk drawer. That was it for the Camping Spell, and everything else I'd snatched by hand on my mad dash out of the manor. Just a small box of trinkets and treasures remained, which I left unopened, in case the floral wards didn't hold... and the book that had earned me a mangled arm.

The binding was dyed with the stain extracted from black walnuts and wrinkled like the flesh of a morel mushroom. An iron clasp kept it latched and its pages free from wear and tear, and a large irregular emerald was embedded in the front cover above bold, silver-embossed letters that spelled out HAWTHORNE. The emerald was a very dark green, maybe even black as it absorbed the color of the cover and reflected it. It was also warm to the touch—that is, *the air* above the emerald was warm. I knew better than to touch that gem. And I should've known better than to touch this spell book, let alone the emerald; only the robed elders of the coven were allowed in its presence.

Which was exactly why someone like me, an uninitiated Hawthorne, had to be the one to do this.

I wasn't tainted like the rest of the coven. And I was wearing a parasite ring, masking my potential to that of a Hawthorne adolescent.

It was so dark. Like living shadow.

My eyelids trembled shut as that frightful memory resurfaced.

From the hallway, my eye glued to the crack in the study door, I watched Aunt Hyacinth and Cousin Otter each touch the stone on the grimoire's cover and a tendril of living shadow rise out in response. They showed no fear as the tendril split in two, reared back like twin heads of a cobra preparing to strike, and plunged into their hearts. Their spines arched, Aunt Hyacinth gasping as Cousin Otter grunted, and then those tendrils *fed*. Beads of green light flashed mutedly along those shadowy esophagi as the thing in that gem devoured their magic, their life force.

Just as it had five days a week, every week since I'd been alive, I just hadn't known until now. Two robed elders disappeared into the study Monday through Thursday, Grandmother going alone on Friday, the coven apparently *compelled* to feed that thing. And afterwards, they acted as if nothing had happened at all. That thing inside the gem was a parasite, a *curse* that fed on my family and then wiped their memories, stealing away their power for...

Exactly what, I didn't know, but when I freed my family of this curse, it would only take a spell or two to determine who'd subjected us to such degradation and humiliation. And what they were planning with our stolen magic.

But first things first.

The spell book and I needed to stay hidden and undisturbed while I figured out just what kind of curse it was and how to break it. And who knew how long that would be?

After a quick confirmation that I was alone, I retrieved my iron chef knife and wiggled a floorboard loose in the center of the hallway.

It would've been better to bury the grimoire under the hearth, but that would be the first place someone would look in a hearth witch's house. The floorboard lifted with a protesting croak, revealing the cool dirt of a cobwebby crawlspace. I sent a tendril of magic into the gloom, and when nothing reacted, I retreated to the hearth for some ashes. There wasn't a scooper or brush to collect it—*Note to self, make a to-buy list*—so I used the broom and dustpan and tried my best not to set the broom on fire. At least the dust pan was metal.

I shoveled the ashes into the hole and dropped the spell book down in after it. Sprigs of rosemary followed, plus another heaped dust pan of ash wood ashes. Ash, rowan, and holly woods were the best not only for protection, but for obscurity. For hiding trails. It didn't matter if it was living wood, deadwood, or ashes. The rosemary caught from the heat, smoldering and releasing pungent smoke, but the grimoire was unscathed from the cinders. It would take more than a little fire to hurt *that* book.

Lastly, I dropped the claw of the Big Nasty on top of it all, a gentle *foom* of a white-gray cloud rising and then coating it all in a fine layer like dust.

With my hands braced on either side of the hole in the floor, I felt that familiar desire in me rise. The itch to release the clasps that held the book closed and unleash those secrets within. I didn't even need the Reisling.

Nope, nope, and nope.

Even I knew I wasn't ready to handle that beastie of a spell book. I wasn't even sure I could read it, though Mom had made sure I knew my runes inside and out. She was the academic of our family, slim and straight where the other Hawthorne women were prone to curves, even me, and often underestimated. Until she picked up a longbow and ruined Dad's record twice over.

Mom. Dad.

All the Hawthorne family members were as a terrifying as they were loving, and other than Grandmother, I feared my parents the most. Or rather, what they could *do*.

Mom, the brilliant scholar who knew more spells than our entire family combined.

Dad, the tracker, who was also the family's combat instructor. There wasn't a quarry he couldn't find, a beast he couldn't kill.

I'd learned from the best, so maybe I stood a chance.

But they'd also taught me everything I knew, so it was only a matter of time until they found me.

Focus, Grandmother's voice sounded again.

Funny that it was the matriarch's voice that kept resurfacing in my memory, the very woman I'd offended the most with my theft.

But you're right, Grandmother. First things first, and second things second.

I waited for the rosemary to stop smoking—it wouldn't do for a cinder to rise and set the underside of the house on fire— then replaced the floorboard and covered the hall floor with the braided rug. Once I'd secured my home, and figured out a plan, I'd be back for it.

Leaning back on my heels, I looked around the empty farmhouse. Not a speck of furniture to speak of. No books, no laptop, just a burner cell phone and charger. The bare essentials, a clean slate. The rest would come.

For now, I lit the wick of a lantern the Camping Spell had packed and turned off the lights to save on the electric bill. A flame lantern was a good deterrent for snooping fae, or humans, especially when cracked across the face with it, so it really was a useful tool all the way around.

Since I had no bed and the weather was fine, I unrolled a thick sleeping bag in what I assumed was the den at the front of the house, fluffed my pillow, and burrowed down under the thick comforter. My back would probably protest in the morning, despite only being twenty-five, but a few days of mild discomfort would be worth it as I adjusted to my new surroundings. *If* I adjusted. It kind of depended on the pixies and whether or not they accepted their new home, or turned *fiáin*. Feral.

Let's hope it's the former.

Interlocking my hands behind my head, I relaxed into the comforting smells of familiar linens and let my eyelids close. Outside, the crickets strummed and the wind swayed through the maple tree.

And then, just as I succumbed to the tug of sleep, a symphony of muted pops.

Pixies, flying into and bouncing off the floral wards.

Just like they were supposed to.

Smiling sleepily, I sank deeper into my pillow. With any luck, the pixies would harmlessly ricochet off the wards and bounce straight towards the delicious scent of bone broth and any sore feelings at their abrupt eviction would be—

CRASH!

I lurched upright at what could only be the metal trash can lid clattering against the ground. Great. So I'd evicted the pixies but had done nothing about the raccoons or opossums that had obviously been lurking around. There was another crash as the trash can was overturned, and then there was an angry whistle.

I kicked off the comforter just as the shrill whistle sounded again, this time *inside the house.* A cascade of ceramic and metal followed close behind.

Dashing into the kitchen, I slapped on the light. "What the—"

Mom's lectures and the myriad books of the Hawthorne library hadn't prepared me for *this.*

Three pixies, each one slim-bodied with silver-green skin mottled with purple, bared sharp silver teeth at me. One had been tearing into the plastic sack around the bread while the other two had been taking turns snatching up the cleaned plates that had been drying on a towel and dropping them into the sink. Bits of broken ceramic littered not only the sink but the floor and counters.

The pixies paused for only a second, like cockroaches startled by a sudden light, before continuing their destruction. The pixie by the bread tore into the plastic sack with its teeth, and the two smaller ones had seized another plate that they struggled to lift to a height that would ensure maximum breakage.

The seven-legged spider by the sink quickly trundled to the safety of the goldfish plant, half its haphazard web already destroyed by wayward chips of pottery.

Dark green magic flared at my fingertips, so easily rising to the shock and anger I felt, but I snatched up a nearby tea towel instead.

"Out, out!" The towel snapped at tiny fannies and legs, the pixies shrieking.

Their iridescent wings buzzed and blurred as they darted out the open kitchen window, dropping both plate and bread to the floor, but I didn't let them go peacefully. I tore out of the back door, bare feet thundering against the porch, and made sure they crossed back over the wards. The protective shield hollowed like a pond swallowing a raindrop, shimmering blue at each point of entry before some unseen force spat them back out on the other side.

"I didn't want to do this," I said, flicking a small sparkling green mote of magic towards the delphinium flowers.

The protective wards shimmered the blue of twilight as the delphinium grew another foot in height, adding another slew of blooms to their spears. These pixies were tougher than I thought. Country strong.

But it should have worked! I'd followed Pixie Relocation Protocol 101 to the *t*: provide a brightly colored replacement home near the current residence, create and maintain a delphinium floral ward around the old residence. I'd even gone above and beyond, adding cotton ball pillows and a gravy boat full of sumptuous broth! And it was *unheard of* pixies breaking through the delphinium wards.

Country strong indeed. Or my parasite ring had affected the flowers' potency.

I waited a few minutes more, the long pink T-shirt with "Flower Power" written on it bunching at my hips under my hands. Flashes of silver green streaked around the birdhouse, but no one tried to breach the strengthened wards. Indeed, most of the pixies were making the sounds of little chimes—happy noises—as they inspected the birdhouse and the cotton ball pillows and the gravy boat filled to the brim with bone broth. There were only a few disgruntled notes, no doubt the three pixies I'd found in my kitchen relaying the *horrors* of their tea towel experiences.

A good enough start, but it seemed those bigger pixies needed extra convincing. "In the rare case evicted pixies should not accept their new home the first night, try tempting them with bright and shiny objects. Lures, if you will," Mom had said. I could do that, so long as they didn't terrorize my kitchen again.

Blowing a faint raspberry, I spun on my heel to go handle the mess of the trash can.

There wasn't much in there except the chicken carcass and the junk and leaves I'd swept up from the house earlier that day. I replaced it all, found a stone in the garden bed to use as a weight for the lid, and returned inside to wash my hands...

...in the sink full of pottery shards. With a sigh, I cleaned those up too, adding them to the trash outside. Emmett's Barn Market would surely have some replacements, and maybe they'd even match.

"At least the night's not a total loss," I muttered, retrieving the bread from the floor. The pixie had only managed to tear a small hole in the plastic bag, one easily knotted over. I put the bread in a cupboard instead of leaving it out on the counter, wondering if it should be secured with the paracord.

Nah.

After a stolen glance out of the den's eastern window—the silvery streaks of pixies still buzzing happily around the gravy boat—I returned to my untidy sleeping bag and pulled the comforter up to my ears. Faint chime-like sounds and the smell of goldenrod drifted in through the window. Maybe the happy pixies could convince those three other bougie ones to appreciate their new accommodations.

And soon. I couldn't tackle the grimoire until I was guaranteed some privacy.

CHAPTER EIGHT

In the morning, there was a dead crow on my front porch.

From the way its neck was bent, I could tell it hadn't flown into my window overnight.

Dark green magic flared to my fingers, becoming briars that writhed up to my shoulders.

There were three explanations for this corvid corpse, and none of them good: a rival supe in Redbud wanted me out and was trying to intimidate me, though I'd only met a handful of people, and they'd all been very welcoming; it was gift from that caliby cat, though I had no idea why that aloof creature would be gifting me anything other than cat scratch fever; or the pixies had chosen to further take out their frustrations on me by attacking the wildlife.

But the hearth hadn't alerted me of an infiltrator coming to my porch last night, and I would have woken at its alarm, so that ruled out the rival. And the bird had no blood on its feathers, plus all its feathers were intact, so it couldn't have been the cat. In my experience, cats were... rough on birds, so it could only be the pixies. No doubt they'd lobbed it through the floral wards.

Again, *unheard of*, and Mom's knowledge was extensive.

Plucking up the poor dead bird by its limp feet, I carried it to the birdhouse, but there were no pixies around to reprimand. The bone broth was gone too. When I peeked inside the birdhouse nesting boxes, I discovered some cotton balls flattened and indented with the shapes of sleeping pixies. So, it would seem, my offerings had been accepted. Mostly. Someone—or some*three*—had scratched off a bunch of paint from the birdhouse.

And had killed this crow.

Slicing my hand through the air, I carved a hole in the ground by the post and buried the poor crow.

Forget bougie, apparently there really were some really nasty pixies in this mix, and the tactics we'd used at the manor weren't working with the same effectiveness. More appeasement was on the docket for today, and that was fine, because I knew a thing or two about pixies. Though I'd never heard of them killing birds before.

Whistling, once again to ward off trouble, I added another chunk of wood to the fire—this time maple deadwood, reserving the rarer ash wood for a once-a-week protection booster—checked to make sure all the windows were open for that gusty crosswind, and set off to town to finish gathering supplies to make the farmhouse my home away from home.

"Back again, I see." Emmett Trinket set the silver candlesticks he was polishing aside and wiped his hands off with a rag. Out of sight, his brownie helper scurried even deeper into the towers of misfit things. "Ooo, and with coffee."

The little bell still jingling, I shut the door behind me gently so as not to release a shower of straw-infused dust from the rafters. I slid the to-go cup onto the counter, careful to avoid the rags and chemicals. A peanut butter cake pop followed, for the brownie. "The least I could do after all your help yesterday.

Cohen at the Magic Brewery said you liked it with a dash of allspice?"

"That I do," the old man said, giving the coffee steam a deep inhale. "Gives me a reason to get up in the morning." He looked over his lid at the to-go cup in my hand. "What'd you get?"

"Double shot of espresso, half a cup of whole milk— steamed—and half a tablespoon of turbinado sugar."

Emmett blinked. "That's, uh, very specific."

What could I say? Coffee orders were like spells. They had to be precise.

"I'm allergic to coconut, and with the anything-but-cow-milk craze going on, I have to be specific. Cohen said he was going to call it the Misty Latte." I shrugged.

"Ah, lattes, the choice of immature coffee drinkers. Drown out all those subtle flavors with milk and sugar."

"Well not all of us like our coffee to match the darkness of our souls," I replied sweetly.

Emmett choked on a sip, coming up from his cup with a chuckle. "You here for a reason, Miss Misty, or just to cause trouble?"

Not in this town. "I thought Ms. Charlotte Harris was supposed to do that."

"Oh lawdy," Emmett groaned, "she didn't fuss about that birdhouse, did she?"

"Never did cross her path," I said, taking a sip of my coconut-free latte. It was delicious, even if it was immature by Emmett's standards.

"Hmm, well, someone no doubt saw that birdhouse on your car and told her, so I should be expecting to hear about it sometime, I suppose. Monkfoot?" he called to the invisible brownie. "Code Imminent Hurricane! Oh, and Misty brought you a cake pop."

"Imminent Hurricane?" I leaned forward, expecting some

gossip. It might not all be true, but it was definitely steeped in fact. And I had to know what trouble I could expect here, which hopefully wasn't that much at all, especially if this Charlotte Harris was a witch or another supe. Maybe my suspicions of a rival placing a dead crow on my porch weren't far off. "Is Ms. Harris really that bad?"

"Physically? No. Emotionally and psychologically? You have no idea." Emmett shuddered. "She can destroy you with a look or be sweeter than a songbird. Problem is, you don't know which one you're going to get. *And* she runs the town paper, *Talk of the Town*, after her husband passed, and while she's yet to publish anything untoward about anyone, I wouldn't risk doing anything to get on her bad side."

"I'll keep that in mind," I said, making a mental note just to avoid her entirely. Then I set down my Misty Latte and rubbed my hands together. "Now I'm here about some plates and some furniture. Whaddya got?"

Since I had only the sedan and no hitch to even attach a trailer, Emmett said he'd arrange for some strapping younger men to come by after business hours to deliver the bed and table set at no extra cost. I'd take the plateware, nightstand, and lamp in the car.

"No couch?" he'd questioned when I had opened my purse to finalize the purchase. "Where are your guests gonna sit?"

The rolls of cash at the bottom of my purse were thinning every day. I had to ration them as best I could until I got the apple orchard up and producing. But I couldn't do that without handling the pixies. And there was the whole moving-in thing. I was going to be here awhile, and that meant I wanted a bed. And a place to sit and work other than the floor.

"They can sit at the dining room table with their tea or coffee," I replied. "For now."

"Better get some cookies or other confections at Galloway's," he told me, shaking his head. "If your guests are gonna have to sit on hard seats while they visit, at least give them something to sweeten the deal."

I wasn't expecting company anytime soon, but I followed Emmett's advice and purchased some shortbread cookies. They were perfect to eat plain, or with a cup of something hot, or even when topped with chocolate spread, jam, or apple butter. When I had these pixies under control and finally got around to assessing the apple orchard and the cider press, I definitely wanted to set aside some time to make apple sauce and apple butter. When I wasn't tackling the grimoire, of course. But I couldn't do that if I couldn't pay the bills. There was a well-established farmers market in Redbud, the perfect place to sell my wares and put a little money in my pocket. Maybe I'd get enough to hire permanent help in the orchard, freeing me up to tackle other, more important things.

"But first things first, and second things second," I said aloud before I could stop myself as I took the exit on the town square rotary that would bring me to Flora's Garden Dreams. I had to introduce myself to the garden gnome running the business and assure her that the new witch in town wasn't here to step on toes or grow some competition. It was only polite, after all.

"I appreciate you taking the time to come back here, what with you leaving like a whirlwind yesterday," the garden gnome said after I properly introduced myself. "And with green juice, too. I'm Flora Ironweed."

"Pleased to meet you. Cohen said you liked the spinach-pineapple smoothie." I stooped to hand the garden gnome the snack-sized plastic cup.

"That boy knows everything, and now he's got your order memorized, make no mistake. He's a beverage wizard, or alchemist, or whatever. A word of advice: he starts making your usual the second you step foot in the door, so if you want to try something new, immediately wave him off."

"Good to know." I'd been eying a caramel latte just that morning, thinking of adding even more adventure to my life, when I'd decided I wanted my usual. It would be comforting, plus it would gauge the barista's skills and ability to follow my instructions. Cohen had not disappointed.

Flora took a sip of her smoothie, nodded approvingly, and craned her head back to take in my full height. I wasn't particularly tall, just five foot seven, but anything to a garden gnome seemed tall. "So, you got an education to go with your green magic, or are you just winging it?"

"I have a degree in botany with a concentration in infectious diseases." Had even saved my family's citrus trees as my thesis. We'd successfully kept them alive north of Zone 9 for over two generations, so I wasn't going to let a little thing like plant lice destroy them.

"And you're only going to be working your cider farm?" the garden gnome asked.

"I'll have my own vegetable garden, too, just for me, and some chickens someday. Maybe. I plan to make use of the farmers market here."

"But no flowers and shrubbery?"

"Just those in my garden for my own enjoyment and p—" I stumbled over the word *protection* and quickly substituted in, "pleasure. Th-they're for me."

Flora sucked in her bottom lip, chewing it as she thought. Her stubby finger, its nail painted magenta pink, tapped against the lid of her smoothie. "Well, green witches are a gentle sort not known for lying, and you're here now, pretty promptly, being polite and whatnot, so I suppose we have an accord." She stuck out her hand.

I bent once more, so the gnome wouldn't have to reach up on

tiptoe, and quickly—but gently—shook her hand so Flora'd have less of a chance to change her mind. Gnomes, of any variety, could be quite ornery if you didn't pay them what they thought was their proper due, and I didn't want to create any waves here in Redbud. Low but friendly profile. People would ask fewer questions that way.

When I didn't promptly turn around and leave, Flora swallowed another slurp of smoothie, then asked, "Something else I can help you with, or did you wanna gawk?"

"I'm interested in your lawn ornament inventory, specifically those glass orbs that have solar lighting?"

"Well, well, well, making nice *and* wanting to buy," Flora mused. "Might just invite you to my sewing circle on Thursday nights. This way, Misty Fields."

CHAPTER NINE

AFTER TOUCHING UP THE PAINT WHERE THE PIXIES HAD CLAWED IT, I staked the blown-glass lawn ornaments around the post of the birdhouse. Mom had said pixies were attracted to bright, colorful objects, and these would be quite lovely in day or night.

I hope. I'd set out another gravy boat of bone broth tonight, just in case.

But before that, I had to do something about this fence. That meant rolling up my sleeves and attacking the panels with some weather-resistant paint. A trickle of green magic encouraged the delphinium border to lean away from the fence so I didn't get paint on the flowers, slowly easing into their upright positions when I was done with a section and had moved on.

Was I avoiding the true reason I'd come to Redbud? Absolutely. *But,* I reminded myself, *you can't possibly tackle that spell book until you're fully healed.* Arthur's salve and my own magic had gone a long way, but I still needed a few days. My magic was rejuvenating quickly, but I was loath to use it on myself any more than I already had, so I funneled it into the amazonite pendant. I kept waiting for the other shoe to drop, which meant I needed to be ready.

And it wasn't just my body that needed healed. My spirit needed it too. After everything I'd learned, the secrets I'd uncovered... I hadn't been as foolish as Pandora that night, but I'd been terribly naïve.

I needed to come to grips with it all, and that meant ignoring it for a few more days while I concentrated on mundane, less violent things.

Sometimes tackling the little things gave you the mental fortitude to then tackle the big ones.

And my "little thing" at the moment was this fence.

Every eight or so feet was a post to provide stability to the panels, and when I approached the third one, my humming tune turned into a yelp.

Remember, I startle easily. I wasn't scared.

The cat was back.

At this point, I was convinced it was just a cat. If it were a Big Nasty, it would've attacked me already. If it were a shifter or a druid, it most certainly had better things to do with its day than remain in feline form and watch me work. At least, one would think.

This particular post was opposite the birdhouse and the new lawn ornaments that glinted in the noonday sun, soaking up energy to sparkle at night. The half-crouched cat divided its attention between the birdhouse and the closest orb, gauging the distance between them, tail flicking.

"Uh-uh," I said sharply, startling the cat as much as it had startled me. Regaining its balance, it flattened its ears, tail still swishing, unamused. "There are no birds up there for you, cat, and that gravy boat is not yours either. Now you're welcome to sit there, but that's all."

The cat just stared at me.

"Well, actually, I'd rather you move so I can paint that post."

The little beast yawned, stretched, making sure every one of its eighteen claws dug into the worn wood of the post, and hopped down into the grass.

"Thank you." The paintbrush made a shooing motion. "Bye now."

I painted the rest of the fence without any visitors, animal, fae, supe, or human, and returned to my picnic blanket for another recharging nap in the sun. Just another day of homey touches and then I'd get to move on to what I'd been itching most to see: the apple orchard.

I could just picture it now: old, wizened branches, the smell of fermenting apples, long grass bowed over with morning dew, old hay composting into the soil. It would be heavenly. But I knew a thing or two about delayed gratification, and first things first, after all. If I abandoned the farmhouse to get started on the apple orchard, I'd never finish my work here. Nor pixie-proof the farmhouse. And then the weight of those unfinished chores would loom in my mind until they manifested into physical stress.

Everything had a season, a time for attention, and right now, that was helping the pixies adjust to their new home. Maybe tonight those three bigger fairies would finally accept the birdhouse and a truce could start to bud between us.

A pulse from the hearth woke me from my afternoon nap. Stretched out on the lawn, I felt the pulse like the tremor of an earthquake deep underground. Not enough to disturb anything, but a ripple nonetheless that made my hair stand on end.

Someone had set off my proximity alarms. Then I heard it: gravel crunching under tires.

A forest-green truck and trailer rumbled up the drive. The driver made a large circle, angling the trailer so its back end faced the farmhouse, and cut the engine. The "strapping younger men" Emmett had commissioned to help move the furniture was actually only one man, but he'd gotten the rest of description right. Especially the "strapping."

Arthur Greenwood stepped out of the truck, a lopsided smile tugging at his mouth as his hazel eyes crinkled at their corners. "Told you it was good to know a guy with a truck and a trailer, miss."

"Uh-huh," was the cleverest thing I could think of, my mind racing like a frantic chipmunk when a cat is near. *The sexy lumberjack shifter is coming into my house! My house with its boxes and bags still heaped by the front door and my clothes hanging up in the back of the kitchen* and a grimoire buried in the crawlspace!

I hadn't much experience with shifters, obviously, and any who met with the robed elders of the coven did so off Hawthorne land, but everyone knew their sense of smell was strong. So strong, Cousin Lilac had told me in a hushed whisper one night by the hearth, that they could scent when women were *in the mood*. That hadn't been the term Cousin Lilac had used, of course.

Thistle thorns! If he could smell something as secret as that, not to mention that single drop of blood on my sleeve, he was guaranteed to smell the scent of rosemary wafting up from the floorboards in the hall. Then it was a one-way ticket on the Suspicion Train to the town of What's Misty Hiding?

But maybe the rosemary in the garden would mask it?

I hurried down the front porch and garden path to the garden gate, snatching up a sprig of rosemary. Who was I kidding? It was practically the entire bush. As I held the garden gate open with a forced smile, I crushed the rosemary in my hand, injecting its perfume into the air. "I-I won't keep you long."

Arthur paused at the gate with two chairs linked on each arm, and I felt that inexplicable pull, that magnetism to be nearer. Sweet, well-mannered, *and* handsome? By the Green

Mother, I didn't stand a chance. His hazel eyes swept from my hands up my arms, an eyebrow arching. "No vines this time?"

Ooo, already with the sass, huh? Maybe he'd be too distracted to note the rosemary. "And interrupt another show?" Those biceps certainly were bursting.

Arthur gave an amused snort and carried on up the front path.

The table and its four chairs went to the tiny dining room to the right of the hallway, and the bed went up the stairs to the master bedroom. Arthur needed no help wrangling the furniture nor the queen-sized mattress up the stairs, so I just followed him around under the guise of holding open the doors, all the while crushing the rosemary like I was wringing a chicken's neck for the soup pot.

And then he did something that made my grip slacken enough to drop the rosemary entirely. Nearly dropped my whole body to the floor, the way my knees suddenly weakened.

He eased the mattress on top of the bed frame, spreading his wide hands across the expanse to brush away the little curlycues of wood shavings that had fallen there. The thought of his fingers caressing not the mattress, but skin and ivy-green satin sheets on top of that mattress, had me catching myself against the doorframe.

By the Green Mother, he's coming closer. Cousin Lilac was right!

Arthur stooped, retrieving the rosemary bush off the floor. He paused in the doorway, a space way too small enough for the both of us, judging by the sudden lack of air, and offered it to me. "I thought I smelled baking bread when I walked in. You making rosemary focaccia?"

"Sure," I gulped. I'd never made that bread a day in my life.

He hummed, but it sounded more like a rumble. "One of my favorites."

I would now make that bread every day of my life.

Then there was that lopsided smile again, but he didn't linger in the doorway. He moved down the hall to the stairwell, saying something about a couch or whisking me off my feet and moving in. His booted footfalls were halfway down the stairs before my addled brain reminded me to chase after him and crush the rosemary.

Emmett apparently had had second thoughts about me leaving without a couch that morning and had sent along a worn loveseat in sage green for the den. Fastened to one of the cushions by a safety pin was a scrap of paper that read, *Welcome to Redbud.*

I'd have to buy him coffee every day for a month—scratch that, buy a small container of allspice and make it myself. The thought had me hastening to the kitchen for the kettle and the shortbread cookies.

"Do you mind if I ask how your arm is?" Arthur asked after a bite of shortbread. The whole cookie could've fit into his mouth, so I wasn't sure if he was taking such small nibbles because the shortbread was bad, or because he was being polite, or because he wanted to linger.

We were out on the front porch watching the sun lower over the fields, mugs balanced on the railing, a slightly chipped plate with a handful of cookies between them.

"The honey salve you gave me is fantastic and the peppermint oil is just the nicest touch, so soothing," I gushed, at the same time wondering how so many words were tumbling out of my mouth. By the Green Mother, what was wrong with me?

I snatched up my mug, slurped down a scalding swallow of peppermint tea, and sputtered. "I-I'm good. Um, sorry. My arm is doing much better. Thanks. And thanks for bringing all this by."

"You're welcome." Another nibble. Then his hazel eyes flicked to my hand. The hand that still held the rosemary.

Why I still gripped it like a talisman, I'd never know—we

were outside anyway, away from the sprig buried beneath the hallway floorboards—so I swept my hand behind my back as inconspicuously as I could and looked pointedly over the railing, taking another sip of tea. And choking shortly after, because I'd forgotten I'd just burned the inside of my mouth.

"Well"—he cleared his throat—"I won't spoil the rest of your evening. Miss." He saluted me with the half-eaten cookie and trotted down the porch steps.

When he didn't turn back around, I groaned.

He must've known about the rosemary, how you grew it and lavender at the garden gate for protection. Wore it around your neck as a last resort. Somehow, he'd known.

Except I hadn't been using this sprig for protection. I'd just wanted to mask the smell of rosemary in the house. Belatedly I remembered I'd used the herb in my chicken soup. Its very scent no doubt lingered in the kitchen even now, probably the whole downstairs. I'd just been paranoid, and now I'd offended him.

But my protest for him to come back and finish the cookies died in my throat. I'd given him the wrong impression, but I didn't want him to stay any longer, either. I had pixies to wrangle and a grimoire to keep hidden and fantasies about lumberjack shifters and satin sheets had no place in my head right now.

"Thanks again, Arthur!" I did mean it, hoping the sincerity rang clear in my voice.

He raised a hand in farewell before entering the truck. That was good. No hard feelings. Or maybe he was just being polite.

When the taillights disappeared down the road, I collected the mugs and plate of cookies and went inside to reheat more bone broth for the pixies. As it came up to temp in a saucepan— I really needed a microwave—I stole a moment to poke my head out the back door. Everything in nature is a creature of one habit or another, and my newly formed habit of feeding the pixies coincided with checking the orchard fence line for those three lumps again.

And they were there, features obscured by the setting sun, grazing deer or woodchucks or whatever they were.

Huh, so I hadn't imagined them yesterday.

Squinting or peering didn't resolve any of their details, so nothing short of traipsing out there across the wildflowers would confirm their identity. But the saucepan was sizzling, calling me back inside so I didn't overheat the broth and burn tender pixie mouths.

When I emerged from the house with their dinner, the lumps were gone and the cat, of course, was back on the fence post. Ears pricked, it chattered like it would to lure a bird or insect within paw-swatting range.

"This is not your dinner, cat," I said, somewhat crossly. This was the second night with the pixies, and the scholars and lectures said that if they didn't accept their new home by the end of the third night, you had feral pixies on your hands that nothing short of an expulsion curse could eradicate. Then they'd be classified as fiáin, wild creatures that would not listen to reason and were prone to be more malicious than boggarts.

Everything had to go well. I had to distract the cat, lest it use the bone broth as bait and snatch a pixie from the sky. The whole pixie community could claim I'd hired feline enforcers and form some sort of union to sue me, *if* they didn't turn fiáin. "If you're hungry, come to the kitchen window." I certainly wasn't going to let it in the house.

Tail lifted, the cat hopped from its post and padded along the brick path, leading the way to the farmhouse. As it diverted to the right to skirt around to the kitchen, I went through the front door. It was the principle of it all; I would not have this wild cat lead me into my own home like it owned the place and not the other way around. The audacity!

When I entered the kitchen, the cat was perched on the open windowsill above the sink, silent as a monk. It had made room for itself beside the goldfish plant, its tail wrapped around its feet as if to keep an errant flick from knocking over the pot.

"At least you're being polite," I murmured, leaning forward to inch the flowerpot over as far as it could go on the sill, just in case.

Above them, Mrs. White, what I had come to call the seven-legged garden spider, had formed a triangular web in the left corner. The spider was in the middle of wrapping a fly in silk, making what I imagined were happy clicking noises. The cat gave it a glance, then looked pointedly at the refrigerator.

"I'm not going to start buying cat food." I went to the stove instead and ladled out a small portion of steaming soup. When it was set down in front of the cat, the little beast took one look at the single scrap of chicken floating listlessly in the meager pool of broth and lifted judgmental yellow eyes.

"Oh, fine." I slipped a bigger piece of chicken into the bowl. "But that's all you're getting."

The cat lowered its head and began lapping.

Pursing my lips, I portioned out more soup for myself, balancing a wedge of bread on the rim of my bowl. I'd had every intention of using my new table and chairs, but with the cat in the open window, I didn't want it sneaking into the kitchen when my back was turned. So I leaned against the counter and ate with the cat, putting both bowls—new from the Barn Market, thanks to those pixies—in the sink to clean when they were done.

The cat, without so much as a nuzzle as a thank-you, dropped down to the porch and vanished into the night. I stuck my head out the window, calling, "And stay away from that birdhouse!"

That night, I forewent the bed, though its mattress was

inviting and it was all made up as pretty as a picture with mauve-colored throw pillows, and returned to the sleeping bag under the den's eastern window. I needed to be alert, and certain thoughts about certain lumberjacks seemed to spring more readily to mind when I was in that room. Plus the bedroom was above the kitchen, in the southwest quadrant of the house, and I wanted to be close to the birdhouse. It would've been nice to stretch out on my new loveseat, but the cushions needed vacuuming.

Soon enough, twilight came with a series of muted pops, considerably fewer than the night before, and the faintest whiff of goldenrod drifted into the house. And, I interpreted from the chime-like sounds, tiny delighted exclamations over the beautiful shiny things around the birdhouse. Ah, pixies, the raccoons of the fae world.

"So far, so go—"

CRASH!

The trash can, yet again.

The kitchen was empty so I raced through the back door, smacking on the switch to the outside light. One pixie, the big one from last night that had been trying to gnaw at the bread, riffled through the trash. It was more mottled with purple coloration than before, and it held the orange-and-white marble in its hands. At the sight of me, it lowered its pointed ears and hissed. But it didn't try to get into the house to cause mischief this time. Instead it hurled the marble down and zipped into the overturned trash can. A moment later it was like a grenade had gone off when all the rubbish shot out like colorful paper from a confetti canon.

"Hey!"

The pixie made a beeline for the closest garden bed. The wards absorbed it again, sending the pixie tumbling back outside the protective barrier where it seemingly limp-flew back to the birdhouse. Streaks of silver and little sounds like flutes greeted it, the pixies chirping happily about the bone broth, the fresh paint, and the lawn ornaments. The rest of them were happy, so why not this one? And what did it have against my trash can? Maybe it was angry about the cat's presence and this was the only way it knew to express itself. The cat had been acting rather antagonistic around the birdhouse.

But how was it getting through the wards? Maybe I was being too soft on them, or maybe that one pixie was just determined to be a pest. Like an angry dog breaking through its invisible fence just to—

The mottled skin! Those purple marks were *bruises*. It was deliberately harming itself for, what? Raiding the trash can? Except it hadn't taken anything. It'd held the pretty marble in its hands and then hurled it back with the rest of the rubbish. The scholars had never said they were petty.

I felt like I was on the tip of understanding something, but it slipped past me like a butterfly flitting around the sweep of a child's net. With flustered sigh, I strengthened the delphinium flowers again and returned to the sleeping bag. I'd go into town first thing and find out more about that cat. And maybe buy a live trap. There was only one more night left to make these pixies accept the birdhouse, otherwise it was the expulsion curse. And magic like that could be tracked. The very thing I had to avoid.

No, the cat had to go.

CHAPTER TEN

"Do you know who owns that cat?" I asked Cohen the next morning as he frothed the milk for my very precise latte. The Camping Spell had included a kettle and a six-shot moka pot, but I needed more than just coffee from the barista who seemed to know everything about everyone. "The one with the white on the underside with red-and-brown tabby stripes on top?"

"Mmm, sounds like Shari's cat. Pronounced *Ah-may*, though it's spelled A-M-E. It's Japanese or something. And yeah, she likes to wander. Why, she been visiting?"

"A *lot*."

The barista looked up from preparing my drink, catching my tone. "Don't like cats?"

It wasn't that. It was the fact that there were *two* more dead birds on my porch this morning, a pair of beautiful mourning doves with broken necks. That darn cat was antagonizing those pixies, and that big nasty one was taking it out its frustration on both my trash can and the local wildlife. If it was one thing I couldn't stand, it was animal cruelty.

"No," I answered quickly, making sure to soften my tone to alleviate Cohen's concern. "She's just been a bit nosey around the, um, birds. But good, I was worried for a second that it wasn't, like, a *real* cat."

"Ain't no shifters around here," Cohen laughed.

"But Arth—" I cut myself off. Redbud was an open magic town, but that didn't mean that every supernatural wanted himself known. While it was clear that Arthur was a shifter of some kind, maybe he was just the hunky lumberjack to the rest of the town. I wouldn't out him.

"Not much around here attracts many mythical folk," the barista continued. "Gnomes, dwarves, and green witches aside. But the *big* supes? Like vamps and weres? I don't even know what this town would do if one of those actually came through. Maybe throw a parade?" Cohen chuckled to himself and snapped a lid over the to-go cup. "Here you go, Misty. Coconut-free as usual."

Throw a parade for a vampire? This barista had clearly not met many vampires... And my pride prickled a bit at the insinuation of being "just another green witch." I was a Hawthorne, albeit a runaway, not that he knew that. But if he did, well, these lattes I'd been paying a premium for would be free. As would anything else in this place.

But I'd left that all, and the pride that came with it, behind for a very good reason.

"Uh, Cohen? Could I get another couple of drinks to go, please?"

The sedan did not have enough cup holders to accommodate six coffees, so it was a game of coffee burn roulette to see if I could balance the tray in my lap as I made the drive down Weaver Lane to the house at the end of the cul-de-sac.

Not to stereotype, but that's a witch's house.

A witch's hat, actually, what with the gray paneling and steeply arched roof of leaf-dusted shingles. Instead of cobwebs clinging between the eaves and covered porch, there were wind chimes and shards of colored glass and dreamcatchers decorated with feathers and tufts of fur and silver beads.

Two rocking chairs were nestled to the left of the door where the porch had been widened into a covered veranda, and two older ladies sat in them, a wide basket of yarn between them. The one on the right in the oversized sweater, forty-something with short brown hair in a pixie cut and wing-tip glasses, had her lips pursed and brow wrinkled as she concentrated on the whizzing of her fingers as she crocheted. *Thistle thorns! Is that a zombie voodoo doll?* She even had a little plastic palette on the table next to her with red fabric paint and a brush for dabbing on fake blood.

To her left was a woman with long white hair braided into a rope over one shoulder, a lilac ribbon woven into the plait that then tied the end off into an elaborate bow. She must've been the one responsible for all the dream catchers, for she was steadily working away on another one, albeit with less rapt concentration than her friend, for she was the one who noticed me approaching first.

"Ah, Misty Fields," she said warmly, letting her dream catcher slump into her lap. "How nice to finally make your acquaintance. And no, I'm not psychic, Redbud is just that small and Flora talks that much. Shari, we have company. Misty's the green witch who took over the old Pemberton house on the other side of the forest."

"Mm-hmm," the other said, not looking up from where she was now sewing on button eyes. Her lips were no longer pursed, her upper teeth sinking into her lower lip as she worked the needle through the button eyes. "Hi."

"Uh, hi," I began, gesturing with the two cups I held in my hands.

"Shari, Misty's brought you a matcha tea."

"Asian pear blend," I added.

"Yummy," she said, still not looking up. She'd moved on to stuffing the head of the doll with poly-fil.

"I'm Daphne Finch," the older woman said, setting her work aside and standing.

There was a shillelagh of blackthorn leaning next to her chair, but the elegant matron apparently didn't need it to cross the few steps to me. She took the cups and set them on the nearby table. Then she enveloped one of my hands in both of hers, a soft smile on her face. I'd never seen eyes so blue before, and from the second she touched me, I felt the faintest *otherness* about her. Somewhere in her faraway ancestry, supe or fae blood had been introduced.

"And this is Shari Cable," Daphne continued. "You mustn't take offense to Shari. She has some compulsive tendencies."

"If I can't craft at the same time as whatever, then I'm not participating," Shari said, once again not looking up from her work. She did, however, pause sewing up the doll's head to take a sip of her tea. "Thanks."

"So, Misty Fields," Daphne began, clasping her hands in front of her belly with all the serenity of a druid priestess, "I suppose you're here to ask after Ame?"

"Ame?" Shari's hands stilled, her brown eyes darting a look to the abandoned cat bed next to her craft table. She pushed her wing-tip glasses further up her nose as if that would help her better see a cat that wasn't there.

"She's out exploring as she does, Shari. She'll be back as always," Daphne soothed.

Muttering, Shari returned to her zombie voodoo doll, stabbing it with red paint.

"You sure you're not psychic?" I asked as Daphne turned her calm attention back to me. "And yes, Ame has been... visiting."

"And you don't want her to."

"I wouldn't mind, normally, but I'm having some difficulties with pixies." My eyes widened at the admission. I'd been so careful at avoiding saying that word, but something in Daphne made me want to tell her *everything*. Not that I was compelled to—I could tell she wasn't weaving a spell on me—but she was just that kind of person. I'd have to be careful in the future.

Daphne didn't seem to notice my momentary panic, or if she did, she kindly didn't comment. Instead, she nodded sagely. "And you don't need a cat's prey drive messing up relations. I assume you've offered them a new home?"

"Of course."

"And made it pretty and inviting?"

"Yes."

"Given them something sparkly?"

"Uh-huh. And I've even given them homemade bone broth every night, and cotton ball pillows!"

Daphne smiled. "That's so thoughtful of you, Misty. It's a wonder why some of them are having such difficulty accepting their new home. You know what you need to do next, right?"

"Expulsion curse," I said glumly.

The elegant matron's blue eyes widened. "Expulsion curse? I was going to say you needed to festoon their house with ribbons. You *do* know pixies are absolute gluttons for ribbons, right, dear?"

"Uh, no. Actually." I guess I'd truly only known *a thing or two* about pixies. Not this third, possibly saving grace, of a detail. If —when—I returned to my family, I'd have to make a few addendums to the books in the Hawthorne library.

Daphne patted my arm like a grandmother would do a child's who'd just learned how to tie her shoe. "Well there you have it. Pixies love ribbons. And horses. But ribbons are easier to get your hands on. And more affordable too."

"But the cat—"

"Ame," Shari corrected, dropping her completed zombie voodoo doll into a separate basket and taking another sip of tea.

"Can you keep her inside for tonight?" I asked Daphne. "I've won over most of the pixies, but tonight's my last chance for a peaceful resolution."

"Why's that, dear?"

"The third time's the charm?" I asked, no longer as confident as I'd once been. "I have three nights to assuage the pixies before it's a lost cause and they need to be, um, *forcibly* removed?"

"Good gracious, what kind of pixies did you grow up with, dear?"

Far less troublesome ones, that's for sure. A Hawthorne said *git* and those pixies got gone. So maybe it was the parasite ring interfering with my authority, or these pixies were just bull-headed, or—what was seeming more apparent—there were gaps in my education.

"Well, we can try to keep Ame inside, but contrary to what most people think, we don't keep Ame. She keeps us. She's a free spirit."

"Okay, well, thanks," I said, unconvinced the two older women, however friendly and sympathetic, would be any help at all. "It was nice meeting you."

"You as well, Misty," Daphne said. Shari just jerked her chin, her crochet hook already busy crafting another zombie. "Good luck with the pixies, and let us know if you need any help."

I don't need luck. I just need a backup plan. And now I have two of them.

Returning to my car, I slipped into the driver's seat and shifted the coffee tray back onto my lap. I took a moment to touch each cup, reheating the contents that had cooled during my unsuccessful parlay with Ame's not-owners. Hearth witches possessed a little command over fire and heat, just enough to stoke what was already there, and after a few seconds, the beverages were as good as freshly brewed.

After a fortifying sip of my own latte, I headed back onto the road and into town, taking the exit for the Barn Market. Emmett had a little bit of everything there, including live traps.

CHAPTER ELEVEN

IT WAS IMPOSSIBLE TO MISS THE SIGHT OF THE FOREST-GREEN truck with its attached trailer parked by the open Barn Market doors. The same rig had been outside my home last night.

Well this would definitely save me a trip to Cedar Haven with my apology drinks.

Old man Cody was in the middle of directing Arthur as he unloaded an ornate hardwood table from the trailer, Emmett standing off to the side of the barn doors and pointing. From the sheen of sweat on Arthur's forehead, it seemed like the table was the last piece in a long line of furniture that had already been unloaded. All three men turned at the sound of my car crawling to a halt in a nearby parking spot.

"Good morning," I called, sticking my hand out of the window and waving. It must've looked awkward and impeded as I balanced the beverage tray on my lap, because both old men immediately barked at Arthur to stop with the furniture and go help me.

"It's alright," I said, even though the drinks threatened to spill as I unhooked the seat belt. "I've got—"

Arthur was suddenly looming in my window. Blocking it

entirely, actually, nothing but a wall of plaid and muscle and the smell of fresh-cut wood. He was in green plaid today instead of red, the same green of the satin sheets I'd fantasized about.

His snowshoe-sized hand and the meaty forearm attached to it slipped through the window. "I've learned it's best not to argue with them, miss. Hand that to me?"

He threaded the tray free of the car and opened the car door for me to step out. *You gotta stop being so nice to me...* By the time I had, old man Cody had reached us, hands outstretched and making "gimme gimme" motions with his fingers. Emmett wasn't too far behind.

"I crave the sweet, sweet nuttiness of— What is this?" Cody lifted the lid. "Green tea?"

"With orange slices and honey," I said, suddenly wondering if Cohen had mistaken Cody for someone else. "Just the way you... like it?"

The old man swatted Arthur in the arm. "You're to blame for this, you know that, right?"

"Doc says you have to limit your caffeine," came a stoic answer.

"I let you order for me one time, *one time*, for the supposed sake of my health, and now that coffee-slinging kid's got it in his head that I live for green tea with orange slices. And he calls this flavorless syrup honey? Bah!" The old man plucked the cup labeled for Emmett free of the tray and stalked off towards the barn in his stooped hunch, sipping and muttering and shuffling his boots. "You're lucky you like yours contaminated with allspice, old man, otherwise I'd be foisting this tea massacre on you."

"Who are you calling 'old man?'" Emmett demanded. "You're the one who walks like a hunchback."

"I'm sorry," I said, but only Arthur heard me as the two older men diverted to the trailer to point and mutter some more. I wiggled the massive cup free of the tray for him. "You like it black with maple syrup, right?"

"I do. And in the big cup, too. You buttering me up for my truck and trailer again, miss?"

Flushing, I set the tray on top of the car and retrieved my own coffee from the car's cup holder. "I actually wanted to apologize. For the rosemary."

"Ah." He took a sip, hazel eyes watching me from over the rim. There was a little flash of amber in them, but I didn't sense any violence. If I had to label it, I'd call it flirtatious. Like he sensed that primal pull I felt to close the gap between us and was inviting me to do so.

I stood my ground. "I-I was nervous."

"Like you are now."

Yeah, but for an entirely different reason. I blushed deeper, hoping to hide it with a gulp of coffee.

"I don't mean to make you nervous," he said gently.

Too late. "H-how did you know about the rosemary?"

"I live in the woods. I'd better know a thing or two so I don't mistake poison oak for hog peanuts." When he winked, I knew I was forgiven.

"Oye, Arthur! This table isn't going to unload itself," Cody yelled. "And I'm sure Miss Misty came to see Emmett, not you."

With a world-weary sigh, Arthur looked around for a place to set his cup, forgetting we were standing in the middle of the parking lot.

I plucked it from his hand and started off towards Emmett. "You can get this back when you're done," I said over my shoulder.

It took only one lunging step to catch up to me. "Holding a man's coffee hostage is criminal, miss."

"You can call me Misty, you know."

There was a flash of that lopsided smile as he shook his head. "Not for a while yet, miss."

"He's old-fashioned like that," Emmett told me, clearly over-hearing. He gestured me inside. "He deliver the furniture alright?"

"Not a scratch on it."

He chuckled. "I'd be shocked if there was. After he found out who he was delivering it to, he packed that trailer with even more moving blankets."

I flushed. "That was considerate of him. And the couch—"

"A gift. And you're doing me a favor. No one's wanted it and it's just been taking up floor space. Pity, as it's quite comfy."

"Glad I could help you move some inventory. But—"

Emmett hefted his cup, the allspice-laced steam fogging up his glasses. "And thank you for the coffee. So, what can I do you for this morning, Miss Misty?"

"I need a trap," I admitted.

His bushy white eyebrows sprouted into his hair. "A trap? We talking poison or live?"

"Live! Definitely live." I didn't want to upset any apple carts with Daphne and Shari—Shari making zombie voodoo dolls on her front porch had made me extra cautious—and I didn't wish any harm to befall the meddlesome cat, but it needed to be out of the way tonight. "Also, do you have any ribbon?"

"Live traps and ribbons? Lawdy, you don't normally see those two things on someone's shopping list at the same time." He chuckled again. "Well, the live traps are in the back of the store, and the ribbons are over here with the rest of the sewing baubles. Arthur!" Emmett raised his hand, waving to get the lumberjack's attention as if he were hard of hearing. "You done with that table yet? The back's not what it used to be, can you get one of those live traps down for Misty?"

"The one for the gophers or the coons?" came a shouted reply.

"What you trapping?" Emmett asked me.

"I'll just go pick out which one I want and come back for the ribbons," I said, already heading towards the sound of Arthur's voice.

"Ah, good plan. Cody, you old toad, stop snooping. C'mere and help me with these baskets."

"I've helped you enough," the carpenter groused, "repairing all that vintage furniture, as if I didn't have my own to sell!"

The voices of the bickering old men faded as I wove through the maze of rolled rugs and armoires, forlorn exercise equipment and farmyard decorations. I passed fishing rods and bait boxes with hooks on display, cast iron skillets and folding chairs, and finally picked out Arthur's looming figure all hazy with dust motes by the rear shelves.

Sunlight streamed in slanted beams through the window, lending a fairytale glow to the clutter. It glittered in his beard and flashed on his teeth, cast the muscles of his forearms in sharp relief between light and shadow as he arranged an assortment of traps down on the floor for my inspection.

"Thanks." I cleared the squeak from my voice. Thistle thorns, it was like I was fourteen and had just discovered Jeremy Rook all over again. Before the Destroyer of Loins had made another conquest, snatching away his attention before he'd even noticed me. "I'll take that one."

Arthur grunted and replaced the one I'd pointed to back on the shelves. "I'll get you another one that's not so rusty. Don't want you cutting yourself and getting tetanus."

"Thanks... Arthur." I said his name softly, almost as an afterthought. Which it was. Calling a person by name drew their attention, and I didn't need any attention in Redbud. Just a quiet place to figure things out.

The brown locks of my ponytail swept across my shoulder as I glanced behind me. I could just barely make out Cody and Emmett arguing about something at the checkout counter.

"Hey," I whispered, gesturing Arthur to join me by the bookshelves where I was spying on them. "Quick, while he's busy."

Trap in hand, Arthur stooped so his head wouldn't poke out over the top row of books. He stole a look through a gap between two hardcovers and shook his head at the familiar sight.

"You know that sage loveseat you delivered last night?" I asked. "Emmett said that was a gift, but it's too much. How much do you think it's worth so I can repay—"

"Uh-uh." Arthur shook his head more fervently this time. "I'm not telling you that. If Emmett said it was a gift, then don't you even think about offering to pay for it. Not unless you want the wrath of the Redbud Curse."

"This town is cursed?" Of all the places in the all the world, I'd apparently decided to hide a cursed grimoire in a cursed town? I inched closer, lowering my voice even more. "What curse?"

"Local superstition, is all. But the townsfolk treat it as real. Gifts given by generous hearts are to be treasured by the recipient, no matter what they are. First, because it's the nice and gracious thing to do, and second, you never know who you might be offending if you don't. Doesn't matter if it's a couch from a nice old man or a bouquet from a friend or a lump of quartz a child found in a riverbed that she thought was pretty. It's never junk."

"But it's too generous!"

Arthur nudged my shoulder with his own. "Nothing you can do about it, so stop worrying. Uh-uh," he said again as I leaned to take the trap from him. "I'll bring it up."

"It's not heavy. And you know I can manage it in more ways

than one. Or perhaps *you* need another demonstration?" Green light bloomed at the tips of my fingers.

"Maybe it's a gift from me to you. A courtesy."

I rolled my eyes. "You're too nice in this town."

"Which makes me think you came from a place that wasn't."

"No! Haw—" I swallowed my protest. Hawthorne Manor was a wonderful place. But nothing was given for free, either. Everything had a price, an exchange that had to be made. "It was just different, is all."

"Well, this is how we do things here," he rumbled, fist tightening on the handle, "so I'll be bringing this to your car."

"Just to my car? Not the house itself?" I snorted.

I'd said it with all the snark I could muster, but from the way he suddenly loomed over me, I was beginning to think I'd said it more like an invitation. My backside thumped against the books as he stepped closer, my hands fisting in my sundress. It was either that or press them against his chest, and I wasn't sure when they tangled with his suspenders if they'd yank him closer or shove him away.

"That depends," he said, voice low. "Will there be rosemary again?"

I blew an unamused raspberry, and the lumberjack straightened with a grin.

"Thought so." He took a large step back and gave a grand sweep of his arm towards the front of the store. "After you, miss."

I snorted again and began the twisty and winding way back through all the mismatched towers and displays. The lumberjack shifter kept pace behind me, and I made a mental note not to wear shoulder-less sundresses into town anymore. They were far too flirty for my supposed low and friendly profile. Which was a shame, really, since sundresses embraced my curves in way shirts and jeans did not.

Mercifully the checkout counter came into sight. It was

smothered in all manner of craft supplies, including ribbons, and the two old men were arguing over something about organizational skills—mainly that Emmett didn't have any, though he insisted he had his "own system."

"You've got yarn mixed with fabric swatches and cross-stitch floss tangled with ribbon and how do you find anything in this mess?" Cody was saying.

"Half the fun is rooting around and finding what you want and discovering other treasures you didn't need but now can't live without," Emmett replied, swatting Cody's hands away from where they picked through a sewing basket. "And how do *you* know cross-stitching thread is called floss?"

"Never mind that. It sounds like you're fostering an environment for impulse buying. You're perpetuating a system of irresponsible spending!"

Just as we were about to clear the shelves of mismatched kitchenware, the last obstacle between us and the arguing old men, Arthur caught my elbow. He yanked me down at the same time the bell jangled above the door.

Before I could protest, Arthur shook his head, indicating silence, and that's when I heard the clicking of high heels.

"This is not good," Arthur whispered.

"What?" I whispered back, shifting closer. My hand found his shoulder to balance myself as I angled for a better look through the gaps between all the rose-colored glass knick-knacks. The feel of hard muscle beneath that flannel was almost enough to distract me from the look of fear on the men's faces. Almost. "Who's that?"

"Trouble."

CHAPTER TWELVE

Trouble wore the shape of an elderly woman in a baby blue pant suit. Everything else about her was white from the hat-and-veil ensemble on top of her head to the pearls at her neck and the kitten heels on her stocking feet. White gloves covered her hands, a white purse dangled from her elbow, and the only splash of vibrancy was the mauve-colored lipstick on her puckered lips.

Backing away, Cody stammered, "G-good morning, Ms. Har—"

"Shoo, Cody Beecham. This doesn't concern you." The spry old lady squared herself in front of Emmett, thumping the basket she carried on top of the counter. "Emmett Trinket," she shrilled, "I thought we had an understanding!"

Emmett couldn't back away as easily as Cody, not with the towers of sewing supplies he'd practically surrounded himself with. He hastily wiped the fog away that had formed on his glasses. "Ms. Harris, wh-what understanding was that?"

"The birdhouse!"

"Uh..."

"You remember the one. The really big one. It looks like a... a bungalow!"

"You mean the three-tiered Colonial?"

"Yes! It was white with sage trim."

"Sky blue with white trim."

She ignored the correction, fussing with her pearls. "No doubt a garish canary yellow now that *she* has it."

It was lemon yellow with rose-pink trim, actually, but at least the old battle ax hadn't deigned to call me a hussy or anything.

"Now Ms. Harris, that birdhouse was bought fair and squ—"

"It was on layaway! For me! Now where are my bluebirds going to roost?"

Emmett bent and rummaged around beneath the counter before extracting a leather notebook. "I can always check my ledger, but I'm fairly confident that I didn't mark that birdhouse as—"

"Of course not! Because we had an understanding." She tapped the handle of her basket. "With these."

His bushy white eyebrows rose as he peered under the basket covering. "With muff—"

"Scones! Yes, of course!"

"Does she ever not interrupt?" I murmured.

Setting his jaw with world-weary patience, Arthur shook his head. His beard tickled the back of my hand where it still perched on his shoulder. I'd found my balance ages ago, so the contact wasn't necessary anymore. And while my time in Redbud wasn't to be squandered flirting with the town's eligible bachelors, especially not with shifters I'd been forbidden all my life to socialize with, my hand stayed right where it was, ignoring my command to release his shoulder.

It was only when my fingertips tensed against my will that I realized I couldn't shift away from him even if my body wanted to obey. His own palm was pressed against the small of my back, the drama unfolding before us having been juicy enough for me not to notice until now. No doubt it was a stabilizing touch, an assurance that I wouldn't lose my balance, crouched over him as I was. And now that I knew it was there, just my cotton sundress separating his callouses from my skin, it was difficult to think of anything else.

Swallowing thickly, I forced my attention back to the one-sided argument going on on the other side of our colorful hiding place. Tried to, anyway.

"Orange and raisin, your favorite," she was saying.

"It is?"

"Honestly, Mr. Greenwood." Ms. Charlotte Harris adjusted her gloves and gave the basket another tap. "I'm going to leave these here and you're going to make this right."

"But—"

"I'll be back in a week," she said with a crisp nod. "And hopefully the *Talk of the Town* won't be running an article about any shady business dealings." Turning on those kitten heels, she marched out of the Barn Market.

I remained crouched over Arthur until I heard the squeal of tires peeling out of the parking lot. It was only when Cody's head jerked from around the shelving with a, "Wussies," that we flew apart.

"You're all wussies," Emmett declared, wiping his glasses off a second time. Then he smeared the handkerchief over his forehead and down his neck. "Leaving me to deal with that harridan *alone*. And she's threatened me with a smear campaign!"

"You put yourself into her sights all by yourself," Cody said. "And despite her threats, she's too classy to run a smear campaign. Rare, for a woman who runs a newspaper. Probably the only nice thing I can say about that old bird." He rubbed the back of his neck. "That said, you know what'll happen if we don't at least taste one of these."

"The Redbud Curse," Emmett sighed. "I know, I know. A

year's worth of bad luck if you reject a gift," he explained for my benefit.

Cody snapped his fingers at Arthur. "C'mere and help him with these."

"Again?" the lumberjack sighed.

"Your teeth are harder than ours."

Arthur pinched the checkered cloth covering the basket with two large fingers and peeled it away as if he was expecting a snake to be coiled up inside. A dozen scones nestled together like fat goose eggs, steam wafting from the golden-hued tops.

"Looks innocent enough," I said.

All three men snorted.

"The last time someone had a *misunderstanding* with Ms. Harris, they ate one of her raisin scones and chipped a tooth," Cody said, rubbing his jaw. "No, no, you get any kind of baked good from that old bird, you cut it open first with a knife and make sure she didn't put any pea gravel in it."

Arthur tore one apart with his fingers. "Seems fine."

Cody prompted him to continue by smacking his arm with the back of his hand.

The lumberjack shifter carefully put a piece into his mouth and slowly chewed.

"Well?" Cody demanded.

"What's he looking for now?" I asked.

"Sand," Cody and Emmett answered together.

"Sometimes Ms. Harris's eyes 'aren't so good' and she mistakes sand for ground flaxseed," Emmett said. "Wouldn't be the first time."

Arthur swallowed. "I think it needs some more sugar, but it's not lethal."

"Well," Cody said brightly. "Maybe she isn't as offended as she makes herself out to be." He clapped Emmett on the shoulder. "You got off light, old man!"

"But what am I going to do about the birdhouse? I'm definitely not asking you to return it, Misty, but she'll be back Friday and…"

"Find another thing to fixate on," I finished with a laugh.

All three men turned to me.

"Misty Fields," Cody began gravely, "that woman's wrath is not to be underestimated."

"Oh come on," I said, helping myself to a piece of scone Arthur still had in his hand. It tasted surprisingly good. "You boys don't see it?"

"See what?" Arthur asked.

"The birdhouse is just an excuse. If she was really upset about it, she would've known what it actually looked like. She just wants a reason to come around and visit. You know, spend time with you?" Cousin Lilac had used the exact same tactic loads of times.

Emmett's jaw dropped.

"Tell me, who was the recipient of the gravel and sand scones?"

"I got the gravel, hence my food taster." Arthur rolled his eyes as Cody slapped his shoulder. "Elmer got the sand."

I leaned against the countertop. "He a silver fox like you gents?"

Cody beamed. "I knew I liked you. And he is."

Emmett cleared his throat. "As I recall, she'd been interested in Elmer's watercolors. Kept coming around the gallery, oohing and ahhing about that one of the waterfall. He sold it to some young thing from out of town during one of the art festivals."

"Yeah, and then she started coming 'round Cedar Haven without buying anything," Cody said, crossing his arms over his chest. "Kept driving potential buyers away from that salad bowl set with the olives carved on it. Told her to beat it."

Arthur and Emmett glared at him.

"I said it nicely," he said defensively.

"Seems like these shady raisin scones didn't start appearing until *after* she was snubbed," I suggested, breaking off another part of Arthur's scone and plopping it into my mouth. Ms. Charlotte Harris was a saucy old lady—she'd soaked the raisins in Grand Marnier before baking. "And did either you or Elmer get smear campaigns, Cody?"

"No," the carpenter realized brightly.

"And since I'd never snub a widow, because I have manners unlike you and Elmer," Emmett told Cody, finally helping himself to a scone, "I don't get scones that chip my teeth. Oh my, these are delightful!"

As I reached for another bit of Arthur's scone, he smacked my fingers away with a playful swat and placed the last morsel in his mouth. A brown eyebrow quirked in a challenge that made my pulse thrum. I feigned ignorance and pretended not to notice when he swallowed and dragged his tongue against the crumbs on his thumb.

"I'm not as new to Redbud as Miss Misty is," he said, "but from what I've seen of this town, it doesn't seem the place for people to be mistaking pea gravel for raisins unless you did something to deserve it. I think Miss Misty's right on the money."

"We're like any small town, magical or not," Emmett agreed. "Exceptionally friendly and yet able to hold grudges for a very long time. But at least we're polite about it."

No sooner did the words leave his mouth did I lurch out of my slouch against the counter. The Redbud Curse, grudges, the age-old "one man's trash is another man's treasure," it all shuffled around in my brain and clicked into place.

I'd offended the pixies! Magic folk evicted them all the time, but I'd done the right thing and given them a new home to retreat to. A trade, if you will, one that had even come with pillows and a free meal. But that wasn't why they were wrecking my kitchen and overturning my trash can at night and killing those poor birds. I'd snubbed their gifts. Those little marbles and colorful buttons and feathers and the shiny thimble. They'd been welcome presents, and I'd tossed them without a second thought. How could I expect them to accept my gift if I'd thrown theirs in the trash?

That large gentle hand came down on my bare shoulder. "Miss?" Arthur asked. "Are you alright?"

"Can you break the Redbud Curse?" I blurted.

The three men glanced at each other.

"I suppose," Emmett began, "if the offender were to seek out the offended in a timely manner, say, a few days—"

"Like three?"

"Sure...?"

I seized the glimmer of hope he'd given me. "Gentlemen, I need the prettiest ribbons. *Now.*"

It was Arthur's turn to nudge Cody. And smack the scone out of his twig-like fingers and back into the basket. "You heard the lady. Start picking out the prettiest ribbons."

"You can have a non-lethal scone when we're done helping her," Emmett said, removing the basket to a spot out of reach behind him.

"But I'm a carpenter!" Cody protested. "What do I know about ribbons?"

"You clearly knew about cross-stitching floss!" Emmett thrust a handful at him to start sorting through.

"If you can see the beauty waiting to be revealed in a piece of wood, you can certainly see it already printed on these strips of fabric," I told him. Twisting behind me, I plucked a simple glass candy dish off the kitchenware shelves. "And this, Emmett. I'm going to need this too."

CHAPTER THIRTEEN

Returning home more hopeful than when I'd set out, I hurried to complete the rest of the day's chores. I'd stayed away from the farmhouse far longer than I'd planned, and there were many things to do before the pixies returned.

After checking on the fire in the hearth—as healthy as ever —I baked the bread I'd started at dawn and gave the farmhouse a good scrub down with lemon-scented Pine-Sol. The loaf I'd baked only a few days ago was almost gone; eating it three times a day would do that. Breakfast was toast with peanut butter, fruit, and a latte; lunch a simple sandwich of salami and Swiss and some baby carrots; then of course soup and bread for dinner. My eating habits hadn't been so birdlike at the manor, but then I'd been eating on the family's dime. Once I got my feet back under me, I was getting myself a ribeye smothered in herbed garlic butter with a side of silky mashed potatoes.

Three loaves went into the oven with the intent on giving one to Emmett and one to Flora tomorrow to solidify our budding friendships. Then I'd look into making rosemary focaccia for Arthur. And Cody, of course, that would just be rude to forget him. Nothing facilitated friendship easier than the gift of carbohydrates.

Then it was time to dig the bits and baubles out of the trash can, clean them off, and display them in the little glass candy dish that sat on the kitchen windowsill beside the goldfish plant. The rest of the afternoon was reserved for the most important task: adorning the birdhouse with ribbons.

The men had helped pick out a fantastic variety in a short manner of time: pink and yellow silks, blue satin, some edged in silver or gold thread, linen embroidered with tiny violets or English ivy. There were dozens more and I hung them everywhere. Two per room, the extra woven through the porch railings, spiraled down the support post, even wrapped around the perching pegs.

When I was finished securing the last ribbon to the base of the acorn finial, I turned to the western lawn to commence my new favorite ritual: the nap in the afternoon sun on the picnic blanket.

Ame was there, sitting in the very center of the gingham, her yellow eyes as judgmental as I'd ever seen.

"I never claimed to be the lead decorator for *Better Homes & Gardens*," I said defensively. "And what are you doing here, Ame?"

The cat made no outward response to the sound of its name, not even a pricking of its ears.

I swept a hand at the bedazzled birdhouse. "Think you could do better?"

As if to prove just that, the cat sauntered across the lawn and jumped to the fence post. But instead of inspecting the ribbons, the cat sat back on its rear paws to angle a look inside the nesting boxes.

"What did I say about that birdhouse? It's not for you!" I clapped my hands, startling the cat so badly it lost its balance and tumbled off the fence post. Oh no! I lurched to the fence and peered over just in time to see a sulking Ame finish smoothing some ruffled fur with a few licks before lifting its tail in a clear snub and sauntering off.

Muttering about cats and manners, I diverted from the picnic blanket to set up the live trap I'd left in the car. I'd bait it later with a piece of chicken and catch the little troublemaker before it could terrorize the pixies.

The afternoon sun had warmed the blanket perfectly by the time I finally flopped down on the ground. A quick tug and a shake made the bandages slither from my arm, letting the sun and grass get full access to my healing wounds. Some more salve and one more nap and they should be nothing more than pale pink scars that would eventually disappear. Tossing an arm over my eyes, I relaxed into the cushion provided by the grass.

"You will not ruin this for me, you stupid cat," I vowed, slipping off into a fitful sleep.

That evening, the cat did not return for supper or the bait in the trap. I ate at the dining room table, the soup and bread somewhat less flavorful, probably because of my nerves. I kept glancing over my shoulder thinking the cat would appear in the kitchen window any moment, but it never showed. Never even yowled to announce its presence, though it hadn't done that before, either.

"Maybe it got the message." I swept the curtains aside so I could peer outside the eastern den window like a voyeur desperate for new fodder for the gossip mill. The gravy boat was full, the lawn ornaments were glowing, and the ribbons wafted in the evening breeze. It was the perfect setup.

The pixies wouldn't come if they knew they were being watched, not until we'd struck a successful truce, so I retreated to the sleeping bag and sat, wrapping the comforter around my shoulders. I'd thought about dragging the sage loveseat to the window, but the now-clean cushions were surprisingly comfort-able, and I didn't want to fall asleep. Not until the pixies had returned. So I sat on the floor and watched the sky for any signs of movement. And if that darn cat came back, I would yank that parasite ring off my finger and slam my hand against the ground so hard the morning glory vines would snatch up that feline pest and drag it caterwauling under the porch and keep it there until sunrise. It'd had its chance to be caught in the live trap and kept in my bathroom overnight.

Despite sitting upright, I must've slipped off into a half-sleep, for I woke sometime later, the slant of the moonlight across the floor marred by the feline shadow that perched in the den's windowsill.

"Ame," I hissed, throwing my comforter aside. "Shoo! You'll ruin everything."

"No, Misty Fields," the cat replied, yellow eyes as disap-proving as ever. "You've done that on your own."

CHAPTER FOURTEEN

"Wh-what?" I didn't know what to be more shocked about, that the cat was talking or that it had told me I'd mucked everything up with the pixies. Aunt Peony had said only a familiar already bonded to its witch, or offering to bond, could speak, and I most certainly did not want Ame for my constant companion. Judgmental attitude twenty-four seven? I don't think so.

"The problem with pixies, Misty Fields," the cat continued, "is that they talk. And since you did such an exemplary job setting up a new house for them, and making them bone broth —which was quite scrumptious, I must say—"

"Thank you."

"Don't interrupt. *And* giving them something shiny to entertain themselves with *and* festooning their house with those garish ribbons they seem to love, well, they've quite talked themselves hoarse, haven't they? Aside from the big one, they've done nothing but sing your praises after the first night. And other things have *listened*."

"What things?" I whispered, finally rising and joining the cat at the windowsill.

"Hobgoblins." Ame finally deigned to look outside, drawing

my eyes to the trudging creature headed out of the misty apple orchard. It carried something in its fist, something it dragged along the ground. A club. Or a hatchet.

Two more smaller creatures followed, no less menacing than the first.

The woodchuck lumps!

I turned back to the talking cat, aghast. "But I didn't—"

"That's *right*, you didn't look any further than your farm-house. You helped the pixies come to terms with their new house mistress, but did you even introduce yourself to the hobs who've worked these orchards for the last three generations?"

No wonder the hearth hadn't alerted me. These creatures had already been inside the perimeter, part of the estate.

"You just took their gifts like you took the pixies' and threw them in the trash!" the cat continued. "Or rather, buried them in the garden. That might ruffle some feathers, but at least you were snubbing them all equally. Then you went out of your way to appease the pixies with all that finery. To all appearances, you're playing favorites!"

The birds! I cringed, thinking of those poor things with their broken necks. Who thought to gift a person with dead crows and doves besides a cat? And this cat certainly hadn't gifted me anything more than a headache. I pushed that thought aside and focused on what was really bothering me, shouting, "If you could talk this entire time, why didn't you say something before?"

The caliby gave me a prim look, so much like a headmistress would a star pupil who was squandering her potential. "They weren't the only creatures assessing you. *I* was evaluating you too, on behalf of my ward, and if I interfered, that would have affected how you reacted and you wouldn't have shown me your true character. You're kind and generous, Misty, a real go-getter, but I must say, you're terribly naïve."

Being raised on a manor estate that you rarely left could have that effect. As much as I wanted to defend myself against this rotten cat, I had to focus on the threat marching ever closer to my picket fence. The floral wards would only hold against pixies, not hobgoblins. "So this is just one big misunderstanding! Maybe if I went out and talked to him—"

"He's carrying a club to bash down your door and take what he thinks is owed him. You think *talking* is going to get you out of this mess?"

"Well it's worth a try!" I lit the lantern and rushed out of the house in nothing but my sleepshirt and bare feet. At the sight of the approaching hobgoblin, who appeared larger with every step, I was thankful for all those afternoon naps. I was at my full strength now, my magic thrumming through my veins.

"Ho, there!" I didn't know how else to hail a hobgoblin. I raised the lantern and waved in what I hoped was a friendly manner. "It's come to my attention that you might have felt slighted or—"

The hobgoblin swept his club, bashing a fence panel into kindling and spraying the flowers with splinters. Stomping steps trampled the delphiniums, the blossoms pounded into paste in the dirt. In the glow of the lawn ornaments, I saw an ugly sneer and a fearsome glint in the hobgoblin's eyes. He had the face of an apple past its prime, sunken and wrinkled, greasy black hair trapped under a long red hat, and a stained tunic covered in leaf mold that was belted around his waist. Like mine, his feet were bare. And unlike me, who'd been roused from bed, he appeared to have sprouted from the forest floor.

Behind him, the two creatures that had trailed him from the orchard were hurrying to catch up. Hobs, if my schooling was serving me correctly.

The light wavered as I set the lantern down on the porch railing and summoned green light to my fingertips. I wouldn't need my iron cuffs for this fae. The emerald green light darkened into the same ivy green of my eyes. It didn't spark with the gold; that only happened when I was happy. Right now, I was mad.

The parasite ring fought to keep up.

"That was uncalled for," I said sternly. "Now state your business and I'll see what I can do about rectifying whatever I've done to wrong y—"

Ignoring me, the hobgoblin turned his sights to the new pixie home, hefting his club.

"Wystan, you wouldn't dare," one of hobs cried out.

The hobgoblin lurched forward with a bellow.

And was met with a yowling ball of striped fur.

The hobgoblin screeched, dropping his club and tangling his gnarled fingers into the furious fur.

"Ame?" I whipped around to the den window where I'd left the cat. And the cat was still there. The one defending the birdhouse was a different one.

"Well don't just stand there," Ame snapped, slashing the air with a paw. "Get in there and help him!"

CHAPTER FIFTEEN

My bare feet *thunked* against the porch steps as I dashed to the birdhouse. The two hobs who had followed the hobgoblin out of the orchard had now reached the hole in the fence. Not woodchucks at all, as revealed by the lantern light, but Fair Folk resembling little men. Dressed like the bigger hobgoblin, they wore long red hats and hunter-green tunics belted at the waist. They looked similarly unkempt, neglected as the orchard they inhabited, but their faces weren't twisted like the hobgoblin's. Nor scratched either, Wystan finally freeing himself of the snarling ball of tabby fur.

He hurled the yowling cat across the yard and snatched up his club.

My glowing fingers clenched into fists.

The morning glory vines leapt from the garden beds, seizing the hobgoblin's forearms and entwining him with spade-shaped leaves and blue flowers. It would take only a thought for the dark green magic to turn sinister, for unnatural thorns to sprout from the vines and bite into flesh.

The thorns of the parasite ring sank deeper into my flesh, curbing my power.

Unlike the other green witches of the world, a Hawthorne embraced both sides of Nature: Life *and* Death. It transformed the color of our magic from the customary springtime green to emerald, darkening even still when we weaponized our power.

That is not *me. That's not who I want to be!*

There was no doubt in my mind that it was our special ability that had made us the targets of whoever had infested our family spell book with that parasite, and I would give them no reason to come after the next generation of Hawthornes any more than they already had.

"Listen to me," I shouted at the hobgoblin, maintaining control. "I'm sorry, alright? Life's been kind of tough lately, and I was just taking it one day at a time, managing as best I could just like everyone else, but I was going to make it to the apple orchard once the pixies were handled! And I didn't know those birds were gifts!"

As I spoke, the vines grew thicker and stronger, and the hobgoblin gritted his teeth, straining against them. His refusal to even listen sent a spike of anger into my heart, my magic flaring in response. The smooth stems pimpled briefly, as if thorns threatened to burst forth, but they didn't. The tourmaline stone in the parasite ring glowed warningly.

"And instead of being a good neighbor and giving me the benefit of the doubt," I growled, "you come here and wreck my fence and—"

With a bellowing battle cry, the hobgoblin tore free of the morning glories, stumbled a step, and slammed his club into the birdhouse post.

It didn't break, the pressurized wood too sturdy to crack under that hampered strike, but it sent a tremor up to the bird-house that rattled the little porch and made the ribbons tremble.

And that's what you get for being indecisive, Grandmother's voice berated. *He never would've broken a real Hawthorne's grip!*

I ignored her phantom voice and watched as the pixies, who hadn't fled from the commotion at all, having preferred to watch the drama unfold, swarmed out of their new house like a cloud of angry hornets.

The closest hob clutched his red hat, yanking it down over his ears, his brown eyes going wide. "Cernunnos' Horns! Now you've done it, Wystan. Let's get out of here!"

The two smaller hobs beat a hasty retreat, but the pixies didn't give chase. They knew who'd attacked their nice new home, and there was a breach in the floral wards, one that the hobgoblin Wystan had made himself. A breach they could take advantage of.

Pixies of pale silver-green glinted like darts as they dive-bombed the hobgoblin. It was unclear if they were biting him or just yanking on whatever they could get their tiny nails into, but the sound was atrocious. Shrieks of the hobgoblin mingled with the chainsaw-like buzz of two dozen angry pixies' wings.

"Get back," Ame ordered, still safe in her windowsill.

I released my hold on the morning glory vines, which had started to tangle anew around Wystan's calves, and backed away from the swarm. Their tiny bodies flashed like quicksilver in the moonlight, and slowly but surely, the hobgoblin was dragged away into the fields that separated the farmhouse from the orchard. Only a moment later, they lifted him off the ground and carried him off.

I didn't know where they were going, but I watched until I no longer heard his shrieks. Then I severed my hold on my magic, gasping as my finger throbbed where the parasite ring clamped on my flesh. The tourmaline stone was no longer its customary purple-green, but a glowing white. I needed to be more careful in the future.

Swallowing past a thick lump that had swelled in my throat, I turned back to my ruined fence and the trampled garden.

The pixies would be furious now, and they might even take it out on me. So it would be an expulsion curse. Thistle thorns.

But they wouldn't be back for a little while, and I had someone to thank. "Kitty?"

The tabby cat had shown exceptional bravery, coming to the defense of my house and the pixies' home against the hobgoblin. I tentatively crept to the area of the garden where Wystan had thrown the cat. "Kitty, are you okay?"

"His name is Sawyer," came Ame's flat voice from the windowsill.

The tabby in question appeared from the thicket of zinnias, one ear torn at the tip and a whole bunch of fur matted. He looked tired, worn down, and surprisingly young. Giving me a slow blink, he rubbed against my leg before trudging to the porch. One hop to clear the railing, another to join Ame in the windowsill. They touched noses, and the older cat immediately started to groom him. "He'll live," she said between licks.

I couldn't say the same about the delphiniums. Not without the help of a green witch.

Pressing my hands against the grass eased the tension from my body just as effectively as a hot bath. It was firm, constant. I guided the green glow of my magic from my fingertips and into the flower bed, the bent stalks straightening and bursting with fresh blooms. It healed the other trampled flowers as well, but there was nothing that would restore the fence except new wood and elbow grease.

Or a cluster of little men.

They had come back, and there were more of them this time.

I lurched upright and backed away, bringing my iron cuffs to bear.

"No, no," their leader said, raising calloused hands. This had been the one who'd pleaded for Wystan to stop his tirade. "We come in peace."

"You sure?"

The one next to the leader cleared his throat in a blatant prompt.

"Is what you said true?" the first asked. "About coming to the orchard tomorrow?"

"As true as rain that falls from the sky." I swallowed. "And I'm sorry again, about the birds. I-I thought they were some sort of intimidation technique."

This time the hob seemed embarrassed. He rubbed at the back of his neck. "Well, it's customary for a hob to give a pair of quail or a pheasant in welcome, but these fields haven't seen gamebirds in decades. We tried to give you the biggest birds we could find. Realize now how the crow could've been misinterpreted..."

While Mom and the other older Hawthornes had been slaves to the education of the younger generations, none of them had ever mentioned the gift-giving customs of hobs. Quite the oversight, if you asked me, especially since that knowledge would have saved me a lot of property damage and hurt feelings. I'd been told they were just the brownies of the fields, farm and orchard caretakers. Without the propensity to be invisible like brownies were. Simpletons who liked simple tasks.

From the intelligent glitter in their brown eyes, there was nothing simple about these hobs, nor their customs and expectations, nor these country pixies, and I was beginning to question more than a few things about my education. Apparently, if I was going to survive in Redbud, I had to accept that all I'd learned at Hawthorne Manor was merely a blueprint, not a fully rendered design.

Thistle thorns. Just one more thing to worry about. But first things first.

"Well, I'm very pleased to meet you," I told the hobs. "And thankful you're more forgiving than Wystan was."

The hobs seemed to accept my olive branch and began muttering amongst themselves—ten, maybe twelve different voices all sounding like the low rumble of faraway thunder—and then something I couldn't hear was decided. There was a sound like sawing, and then one hob produced a hammer, another a bag of nails, and I realized they were going to mend my fence.

"We'd paint it too, if you've got any left over from yesterday," the leader said.

So they'd been watching me. "In the shed. This way."

Two hobs broke off from the pack that had started to cut planks to length, respectfully coming to the garden gate to be allowed entrance instead of trudging through the flowers I'd just healed.

As I handed over the paint bucket and the paintbrush to the second hob, I invited the leader up to the porch and turned on the outdoor light. The hobs murmured appreciatively that they now didn't have to work in the dark, and the hob leader seemed to approve of the gesture as he removed his red hat.

"The name's Roland," he supplied.

"Misty Fields." I stuck out my hand.

He seemed startled by the gesture, and in fact, the hob posse had all ceased their work, mouths agape.

"I'm sorry," I said, starting to withdraw my hand. "Did I do something—"

The hob seized my hand in his own weathered one, giving it a hearty shake. "No. We're just not used to being seen as anything but the help. The last owners, the Pembertons, were even afraid of us. We just work the orchards, ma'am. We don't do anything nefarious."

"Except Wystan." My gaze drifted from the working hobs to the direction where the pixies had carried him. They still hadn't returned to their birdhouse. "Do I have to worry about him?"

"Wystan was a bully and a thief," Roland spat. "He shamed the hob name, his greed twisting him into a hobgoblin. That was an awful way to go, but we're glad to be rid of him."

The other hobs, who were all working on the fence and presumably not listening, all muttered in agreement. I swallowed nervously, wondering just what sort of pixies I was housing. Butt-whoopin' pixies, it seemed.

"He ain't dead," Roland clarified, his voice low. "Just probably gnawed on a bit. Those pixies will be better than pit bulls if he comes 'round here again to start up trouble."

"That's a relief."

"They've got nothing but nice things to say about you, ma'am."

"Except the big one," I muttered, though I brightened quickly. "I have a plan about that one though. If she or he is amicable."

The hob looked up at me with approval in his brown eyes. "That delphinium border was the humane way to go. Just a little bump on the noggin to keep 'em clear, then redirected to that bone broth and that fancy new house with all the trimmings. They love it."

There was a pause where I wasn't sure what to say. One of the hobs coughed, indicating that they were finished, and from the smell of fresh paint, they certainly were. But they didn't leave.

Roland gave an expectant blink, dark lashes sweeping against his tanned face.

Thistle thorns! Where were my manners? "Won't y'all come in?"

CHAPTER SIXTEEN

THE HOBS, AND THERE WERE TWELVE OF THEM, CROWDED AROUND my dining room table. As they were all less than three feet high, they could easily sit two to a chair, bare feet dangling above the floor. The rest pressed around the table's edge, kind faces and brown eyes sparkling with excitement. Ame and Sawyer had exchanged the den windowsill for the one above the kitchen sink, and in her special corner, Mrs. White tended to the fly she'd caught.

At the head of the table, I sliced thick slices from the loaves I'd made earlier that day. I could make more for Emmett and Flora tomorrow. There wasn't enough chicken soup or cookies to distribute, but the hobs seemed pleased as punch with just the bread.

One of the hobs let out a low moan. "We've been smelling that all day. It's even better in person." He cast me a beseeching look as he withdrew a cloth-covered crock from the pouch on his belt and set it on the table.

"Dale, don't be rude," Roland whispered.

"You don't mind, do you, ma'am?" Dale asked, removing the cloth lid. "There's enough to share."

I recognized the smell immediately. "Is that... apple butter? And please, Misty's just fine."

He pushed the crock proudly towards the center of the table. "Made fresh this season."

"Knives are in the drawer right of the sink," I told him. "I slice, you spread?"

Beaming, the hob scurried off to the kitchen and returned with a butter knife and got to smearing apple butter on the bread. And when every hob had his bread and apple butter, Dale made sure to heap all the rest onto my slice, a least a half inch thick.

I groaned as the first taste of caramelly apple butter hit my tongue. There was brown sugar and cinnamon and all the goodness of sweet apples after being cooked low and slow all day. Dale gave me a knowing smile and dug into his slice. The twelve hobs and I munched on our midnight snack, little grunts of happiness drifting up from the table, proving the old saying that nothing facilitated friendship easier than the gift of carbohydrates.

From the kitchen windowsill, Ame gave a small, prompting meow.

"Oh!" I stuffed one more bite into my mouth before abandoning the snack on the tablecloth and hastening to the kitchen.

"I'm so sorry." At least I hadn't forgotten to smear the young tomcat's wounded ear with salve. The soup I'd been reheating for them was simmering and steaming; it was time to eat and the cats didn't want to wait another minute. "I suppose I should thank you for the *belated* warning, Ame, and you, Sawyer, for the help. Ame, is that why you kept looking into the birdhouse?"

"I was looking for a pixie to threaten into keeping his or her mouth shut about your renovations and to tell the others to do the same," she said flatly. "They were riling up the hobgoblin every day. Especially after you buried that crow."

"Like I said before, you could've just told me that," I replied in the same tone.

"I'm a cat," Ame replied, licking her paw. "I don't have to explain myself to you."

"Uh-huh, well, don't feel like you need to keep your thoughts to yourself next time." I poured the gently steaming soup into a bowl and set it in front of the cats. Ame didn't partake, but the young tabby tomcat eagerly started to lap it up, purring the entire time.

"So," I began nervously, "does this mean you want to be my familiar now or something?"

Ame's ears flattened. "Your what?"

"Familiar?" Was I pronouncing right? There wasn't a Gaelic twist on it I was forgetting? "You know, because you're talking to me?"

"You think that because I'm deigning to speak with you I want to bond with you? I already keep a few humans. What makes you think I want to add you to the litter?"

Yet another gap in my preconceived notions. Guess while I was out here I should start my own notebook of observations and knowledge, if not only for my benefit, but for the rest of the Hawthornes too.

"That's just what I was taught," I mumbled lamely. Though I was relieved Ame wasn't interested in me.

"How arrogant," the cat mused, though there was no reprimand to her voice, just an observation. Then she arched her back into a deep stretch, the matter forgotten. "Like I said before, this is Sawyer. My ward. Like you, it seems, he is in need of a fresh start. I figured you two could... look after each other? It's that or he takes his chances at Daphne's animal shelter, and I much prefer my feline brethren in good homes. Even if their owners are a bit slow on the uptake."

Sawyer winced, and I pursed my lips.

But I only had to give it half a second's worth of thought. Have a companion, one to (eventually) trust my secrets with so I didn't feel so alone? While this talking Ame cat was barely tolerable, her ordinary ward Sawyer seemed much more endearing. Maybe that was the difference—the ability to speak just upped their cattish churlishness. And I owed Sawyer for helping me with Wystan. "I could do that."

Sawyer looked up from his dinner to give me another slow blink. A mark of trust in the cat world.

"Looks like you'll be buying cat food after all," Ame mused. "Well, bye now."

And she disappeared into the gloom.

"We should be going too," Roland announced from the dining room doorway. He placed the long red hat on his head, smothering his brown hair. "Work starts at daybreak, just as always."

"I'll see you tomorrow?" I asked. "In the apple orchard?"

He bobbed a nod, a smile flickering over his face. "We'd like that, ma'am. C'mon, boys. Need our beauty sleep an' all that. Dale, don't forget your crock."

The hobs all murmured a farewell and marched out the front door. There was a shuffling of feet, then a hob was calling over his shoulder, "The pixies are all back, ma'am. Snug as little bugs in a rug."

"Thank you!" I retrieved the glass candy dish from the windowsill as well as Arthur's salve. Then I was out in the east garden, calling to the pixies.

"Sorry about before." I hefted the dish of trinkets as I neared the birdhouse. "I didn't realize these were little gifts, but thank you! They're on display in my kitchen. That's a place of honor in a hearth witch's home. The big one, I don't know your name, but will you come out?"

There was a discord of chimes—the pixies clearly chastising

one of their own—and then the big silver-green fairy poked its head around the side of the house. The mottled skin had faded, but what bruises remained looked sore. Its purple eyes gave me a wary look.

Slowly, so as not to startle it, I placed the candy dish on the ground and unscrewed the lid off of Arthur's salve. "This should help with the bruising. If the other two are still bruised as well, they can use some too."

When the pixies—for many more were watching—didn't flee, I stepped closer, reaching beyond the delphinium ward to nestle the jar on the birdhouse porch. Before I could withdraw my hand, the big one zipped to land on the edge of the jar, seizing my index finger with both hands.

I tensed. Fairy bites stung something fierce, but it had every right to bite me for the disrespect I'd shone its and the others' gifts. Maybe that's what it would take to settle the score between us and start fresh.

But the pixie, purple eyes solemn, just pumped my finger up and down with both hands in imitation of my handshake with Roland. I beamed a smile at it, the little creature baring a row of sharp teeth in response.

When released, I retrieved the candy dish of trinkets and gave them a wave. "Night, now!"

Happy chime-like voices and the scent of goldenrod followed me back into the farmhouse.

Sawyer was licking his bowl clean, very thoroughly, when I entered the kitchen.

I waited for him to finish before extending my fingers for an introductory sniff. His whiskers tickled my skin, and then he lowered his head, asking for a head scratch. Yes, much more endearing than Ame. His young fur was still soft, and a loud purr emanated from his chest as I scratched behind his ears.

"Whaddya say, Sawyer? Wanna come to the apple orchard with me tomorrow?"

The tomcat leaned further into my touch, simply purring.

"No angry hobgoblins, no insulted pixies—it'll be a break from our recent adventures. It's time for a little normalcy, right?" I chuckled to myself. "Heh, at least you're an ordinary, non-talking cat."

Sawyer lifted luminous amber eyes. "And that, human, is where you're entirely wrong," said the cat.

EPILOGUE

IT WAS DAWN WHEN AME LEFT THE COMFORT OF THE CAT BED ON Shari's porch and strolled towards the forest. She would have preferred to doze until the morning sky of streaky pinks and purples had cleared away into the full blue of an autumn afternoon, but there was still so much to be done.

When she came to the edge of the property, where the dewy grass met the tree line, she paused to stretch. Ame was no youngster anymore, hadn't been for the last seventy-five years, and there might be something in the woods with the gall to chase her. With that in mind, she finished her stretching by clawing the nearest cedar tree, sharpening her nails to needles in the process. Sufficiently limber, she disappeared into the forest.

Whiskers twitching and nose sniffing, she soon located a water source. A little puddle at the rooty base of a sycamore, actually, and in true cat fashion, she feigned disinterest as she surveyed the area for anyone and anything. Just a squirrel or two in a faraway tree and a bunch of birds all atwitter, but nothing nefarious. Nothing *other*.

After finding a barbed length of briar, she circled back to the puddle and pawed at the water to remove the stray leaves and other debris until the surface was clear. Then she rocked back onto her haunches, slammed her right front paw down on the briar thorns, and said in a low but clear voice, "*Aqua lumosa reflecta.*"

The incantation set the puddle to shimmering, smoothing into a glassy sheen and revealing another cat on the other side of this magical window. A silver lynx crouched over an open book, squinting at a page as an enchanted quill scribbled away. It took only a fraction of a second for this scribing cat to realize it was being watched, lifting piercing blue eyes that still made the fur on the back of Ame's neck stand straight up even after decades of working together. While the president of Grimalkin University had many jobs, one of the most important ones was being absolutely terrifying. How else would she defend her students and staff against arrogant witches, warlocks, and mages?

"Ame Roamer," the lynx said, no inflection whatsoever present in her voice. She was neither delighted nor annoyed at being contacted, just all business, like always.

That's good. She doesn't know. Ame inclined her head. "Fanga Longclaw. I have an update on the familiar trainee Sawyer Blackfoot."

"Ah." The enchanted quill immediately lifted from the paper, and the pages flipped until the appropriate entry was found. The quill hovered by Fanga's ear. "Proceed."

"I have initiated a field switch due to familiar-witch incompatibility. Sawyer's new partner is—"

The quill stopped writing as the president said, "Incompatibility? You're sure? There hasn't been an incompatibility, well, since you."

Ame's tail had started to twitch; she wrapped it tightly

around her body, hiding her front paws. Keeping her voice civil, she replied, "I'm aware. But my assessment stands."

Tufted ears pricked and blue eyes wide, the lynx stared at Ame, doing her own assessment. Ame kept her expression neutral, perhaps a touch on the disinterested side, though her heart was beating as fast as if she'd just chased a rabbit. Not one word she'd said was a lie, but if Fanga Longclaw pressed her for more details, she just might. And that silver lynx could sniff out dishonesty faster than a hummingbird could beat its wings.

The lynx blinked, her assessment over. She returned her attention to her book. "First name?"

"Misty."

"Last name?"

Here Ame pressed down on the thorns some more. "Fields."

"Hair color?"

"Black."

The quill made a note and paused again. "Eye color?"

"Blue."

"Body type?"

Ame eased up on the thorns. "I believe the human world would call her curvy."

"Noted." The pages shuffled again, presumably to the place they'd been before Ame had called. "As Sawyer Blackfoot is still a student and on trainee leave, and what with this field switch, I expect updates every two weeks. His pass has been renewed for another six months. Either he binds to Misty Fields and completes his education from home, or he is returned to the university for evaluation."

"Understood."

"I trust this increase in reports won't interfere with your other responsibilities?"

"No."

"Excellent. In the meantime, I will research this Misty Fields."

Ame felt her stomach sour as if she'd just lapped up a bowlful of spoiled milk, but she didn't twitch a whisker. Witches were numerous and as wide-spread at wildflower seeds. It would take Fanga many weeks, if not months, to discover a witch named Misty Fields didn't exist.

Fanga Longclaw looked up from her book and nodded once. "*Cara dílis.*"

Faithful friend, the motto of Grimalkin University.

"*Cara dílis,*" Ame replied, and the magic window vanished.

Taking care not to limp, she walked away from the puddle. When she was out of sight of the water, she sat down heavily and licked at the wounds on her paw. Like a human with a thumbtack to trick a lie detector test, she'd used the briar to fool Fanga. It'd been risky, and only time would tell if she'd been successful.

Hair the color of fertile loam, eyes the green of the ivy that crawled up the western wall of the manor, this Misty Fields was a Hawthorne hearth witch and no mistake. While "Fields" was certainly an alias, she wasn't sure if "Misty" was. The naming tradition of the Hawthorne coven dictated flora for the females and fauna for the males, but "Misty" was still in the Nature realm of possibilities. It'd been decades since Ame had been welcome at Hawthorne Manor, maybe they were naming subsequent generations after water sources now.

Either way, Ame would keep Fern Hawthorne's grandniece's identity a secret. She had fled Hawthorne Manor under a false name for a very good reason, wearing that tourmaline parasite ring to obscure her magical signature, and Ame owed it to her old mistress to help Misty as much as she could. She'd have to tread carefully, though, inferring only when necessary, as she had with the pixies. No one could suspect there was anything special about her.

"Perhaps she'd the one foretold to break the spell," Ame mused, picking her way out of the forest.

She climbed the porch steps and returned to her bed to clean her wound one last time before curling up for a morning nap. With Misty in hiding and it only being a matter of time before the Hawthornes discovered her—for they most certainly would—Ame would need her strength for what was to come.

The End of *The Problem with Pixies*.

WANT MORE?

Misty and Sawyer's witchy small-town adventures continue in Book 2, *The Cider Hex*.

You can also get access to behind-the-scenes content including sneak peeks, freebies, and all bookish updates by signing up to Kat's newsletter:

www.subscribepage.io/HomesteaderHearthWitchBooks

OTHER BOOKS BY KAT HEALY

Delta Underground Operatives Series

The Case Files of Eryn & Larcen

(series complete)

Hunter's Curse

Avenging Blade

Broken Stars

Soul Reaper

The Paradise War Series

Apocalypse Dance

With Ramy Vance in the GoneGod World

(series complete)

Kidnapping Phoenixes and Other Ways to Die

An Infernal Heist (short, available in Trampolining with Dragons)

ACKNOWLEDGMENTS

Thank you, Lord, for getting me here, then giving me the strength and focus to see it through.

Thank you, Matthew (for all the ways you give me encouragement and support—your unfiltered input always makes for dialogue gold), my family, friends and colleagues (Brandy and Melissa, Jenn and Shavonne, Robyn & the Scribes, the Wednesday Mastermind), Diane (who meticulously and gleefully proofreads these stories), and of course my loyal Wagtail Collective. Kitty and doggo snuggles are the best, plus the walks you require me to take you on keep me from going blind at the computer.

ABOUT THE AUTHOR

Kat Healy is an "all the fantasies" author living in the Midwest, USA with a bunch of cats and one fantastic hound dog. When she's not converting her acreage into an orchard or trying to coax vegetables out of that red clay soil (her green thumb is rather an anemic chartreuse), she enjoys kayaking and snorkeling, watching action movies and baking all the things that are really good at ruining weight loss goals.

Join her on Social Media!
Facebook Author Page: Kat Healy Author
Facebook Reader Group: Kat Healy's Magical Book Café
Instagram: @kat.healy.fictioneer

Made in the USA
Thornton, CO
12/02/24 13:51:24